i

Serious Leigh
Melanie James

BESTSELLING AUTHOR

MELANIE JAMES

Serious Leigh

Book 2 of the Literal Leigh Romance Diaries

Table of Contents

Praise for Melanie James

A Valentine's Surprise - "It was one of the cutest and hottest novellas I've ever read. It's rare to have such a great mix of cute and hot, but this author does it perfectly!" ~ Willow Star Serenity Reviews

A Valentine's Surprise - "This is one of the best short stories I have read in a long time!" ~ HeadTripping Books

A Valentine's Surprise - "This little love story is capable of getting your juices going and turning a dull afternoon into a page turning glorious day." ~ Aubree Lane, Author of Sierra Mist & Early One Morning"

Conjuring Darkness - "I was already a huge fan of author Melanie James so I expected her to write another amazing book. Even I didn't expect how incredible Conjuring Darkness would be. I couldn't put it down!" ~ Kelly Cozzone, Author of Tropical Dreams

A Valentine's Surprise - "Kuddos to Melanie James for throwing a good romance our way. I want more!" ~ Jennifer Theriot, Author, Out Of the Box Series

Conjuring Darkness – "Conjuring Darkness captivates your attention right from the start and never let's go. The adventure packed into this supernatural thriller only keeps you on the edge and turning the page. It definitely was one of those books that was hard to put down." ~ Angela Ford, Author of Closure

Conjuring Darkness – "This book is captivating from the first page, I could not put the book down. I was so surprised by all the twists, turns, the unexpected. I could not wait until I was through each chapter." ~ Angie at I Heart Books

Hot reads by Melanie James

Literal Leigh Romance Diaries
Accidental Leigh
Serious Leigh
Hopeful Leigh
Haunting Leigh

Éveiller
Ava & Will
Kara & Dave
Laura & Alan
Jamie & Brad
Ashley & Jeff
Valerie & Greg

Stand Alone
Beautiful Betrayals – TBD

Darkness Series
Conjuring Darkness
Hour of Darkness – TBD

Seasons of Love Series
A Valentine's Surprise
A Summer Love

The Paranormal Plantation
TBD

Edition License Notes

Copyright

Acknowledgements

For all of my readers, you are the best! Thank you!
Monkeys – Old and new, thank you for always being there for me!
PTCLS – The continual support, love, and laughs you all provide is amazing. You girls have become my sisters. I don't know what I would do without each and every one of you!
To my kiddos - Thank you guys so much, for not staging a rebellion and giving me the time I needed to get this book finished and out!
To Ron – You are amazing and I love you more than life!
Alicia – Thank you for taking the time to clean everything up!

Dedication

This book is dedicated to all women, no matter where you are in the world. Be Strong, Stay Strong! You are worth it!

Chapter One
The Witches Union Local 1313

The cloud of smoke began to clear and my coughing fit finally settled down. Luna was tight against my chest with her claws piercing my arm. We looked around and saw we had been transported to a room in an old building. It reminded me of a bank or post office from the late 1800s. It appeared to be a reception area that had a completely Victorian look. In front of me was a large ornate wooden desk that had a beautiful young woman seated at it. She couldn't have been more than thirty years old. Her long red hair was pulled up and off the shoulders of her pinstripe business suit. Her thick, black frame glasses were really the touch for the naughty librarian look, and she sure nailed it. It helped that her tight fitting suit coat had only two buttons barely keeping the thing on.

"Hello, Leigh. Hello, Luna. My name is Esmeralda. Please, have a seat until you're called."

"Hi—Esmeralda. I can't say I've heard that name before. So, what exactly is this place?"

"The Witches Union, Local 1313, of course. And the note you received wasn't just an invitation, sweetie. Think of it more like a summons."

I was thinking she looked a little young to be referring to me as sweetie in such a condescending tone. She sounded like my mother.

"Since you're so curious, I'll tell you. I'm 326 years old." She scrunched up her face and then added "sweetie."

"What! You can read my mind? And I don't know what's more incredible! The fact that you can hear my thoughts or that you look so young for a 326 year old. I don't know what beauty products you're into, but you need to share the secret." I paused to gauge her reaction and I was happy when she smiled at me. "Also, what exactly am I walking into here?"

"Listen, Leigh. I'll give you some advice. When you go in there, be polite and respectful. Those are some real old-timers in there."

"What do you mean?"

"You are going before the review board. They are going to check you out to see if you are worthy of being a witch, but don't worry. You never would have made it here if you didn't have something they wanted. God only knows *what* that could be." With her hands on her hips, she looked me up and down. "Just remember, despite what they look like, they are several centuries old, and they aren't always very nice to young—rookies." She looked me over once more, and she seemed less than impressed at what she saw before adding a snarky little quip. "Like you."

"Okay. I'll remember that. Now, *where* in the world are we? It's hotter than hell in here."

"New Orleans. Yes, it is hot. And you are far too underdressed for hell, my dear."

"Uh—of course." I started to think that perhaps I fell and cracked my head, hard. So hard that I was actually lying unconscious in my living room, dreaming all of this.

"No, you're not dreaming, and it looks like they are ready for you now."

I stroked Luna's fur and spoke softly to her. "Well, the crazy train is about to leave the station. Might as well enjoy the ride." Esmeralda opened a heavy wooden door and ushered me through. It was a very upscale boardroom. The kind of room you could imagine seeing extremely rich and ruthless Wall Street types plotting their next financial calamity. Instead, three women were seated at a long wooden table. It's not like they were in the stereotypical witch's costumes. These ladies wore little black cocktail dresses and looked quite elegant. Elegant and stunningly beautiful women, no more than forty years old. They looked as if they should be milling about in an upscale art gallery on opening night. I imagined them strolling around with the cream of high society, saying things like, "Thank you, dahhling." You know, saying the word darling in a way that just made them seem snooty. I glanced down at my summer ensemble of a tank top, shorts, and worn but comfortable old slippers. I chuckled out loud when I realized how underdressed I was. I felt slightly awkward, but it's not like I had a chance to prepare for the meeting. Trust me, I've been dressed worse for a midnight run to Walmart and I wasn't going to let this phase me.

The woman in the center flashed a comforting smile. She had long flowing curls of red hair and emerald green eyes. She introduced herself.

"Hello, Leigh! We are so happy to finally meet you! My name is Hilda, this is Isabel, and Marie." She nodded to the women on either side of her.

The woman to her left had a full head of long curly blonde hair and bright blue eyes. Her curvy look screamed sexiness. She was very beautiful, and her little dress strained to contain her huge boobs. *Holy cleavage! And those look real!* I thought. She laughed and said, "Hi, Leigh, nice to meet you. And yes, they are all natural." She winked at me. Thank God, she had a sense of humor.

On the other end was a tall and slender African woman, she looked at me with a very stern gaze and then smiled warmly. It took me a minute to place her accent. *Creole?*

"Ah, Leigh. Our new young writer. I am so pleased to meet you. We all are. I must say, we have been waiting a long time for a writer. Isn't that right sisters?" She looked at the other two.

"Yes, we certainly have. We'll talk more about that in a bit. First things first. Leigh, I know you had no idea that we exist or that all witches belong to a union. So, we have decided not to reprimand you for the unapproved use of witchcraft. However, we will require you to join the union and pay dues."

I began to sweat a little. A teacher's salary isn't exactly the gravy train. I hadn't been very good at balancing my checkbook either. I was to the point where writing a check made me hesitate to hand it to the cashier at the grocery store, and I always breathed a sigh of relief when they ran it through the little verification gadget in the cash register. "Dues? How much are we talking about here?"

"Well, if we go back to the point where you got the desk, it comes up to six dollars and thirty two cents."

My mouth almost hit the floor. "That's it? Really? You had me worried for a minute."

"Well, these rates were set a long time ago, a very, very long time ago. It's really just a matter of principle. I'm sure you understand."

"Oh, yes! Of course." I was more than agreeable to their dues.

Hilda spoke up. "Let's cut to the chase here, shall we? You are the first witch in decades that has the writing power. We all have our specialties, and you happen to be one of the few that can make the magic desk work."

Isabel added, "Yes, Leigh, it's a very important power for us. We got a look at that story you have started. Let's see—I have the title written down somewhere." She shuffled through a small notebook. I cringed with embarrassment, because I wasn't sure if they were going to laugh their asses off at the title I had chosen. "Ah ha! Here it is." She cleared her throat and then announced it loud and clear. "Four Bitten Fangtasy."

There was a crazed cackle and a snort from behind me. I turned my head to see who it was and there was Esmeralda, the Naughty Librarian. I had no idea that she was still in the room. "You're kidding, right?" Asked Esmeralda.

"No. No, that is the title she has. I'm sorry you don't approve, Esmeralda, but we love it."

"Umm, is there any special reason that you are interested in my story? Because, seriously, it is nothing more than a sort of fan fiction. Well, more like payback against the author of my favorite series. I never intended for it to be anything substantial."

"Oh, we are all fans of paranormal romance books. I mean, why wouldn't we be?" They all chuckled.

"Yes, I just love the werewolf books, personally. I can only speak for myself when I say I am hoping for a book that finally gets it right. And let me tell you something, honey, once you've tried werewolf, you'll have a whole new appreciation for the word stamina!" Isabel said.

"Seriously, Isabel? Werewolves stink and all they want to do is doggy style. Now, let *me* tell you something when it comes to fucking around with a werewolf, *protection* has a whole new meaning." Marie chimed in.

Hilda joined in, "You've got that right, sister, a flea collar, that's the protection you'll have to insist on. And don't even get me started on how they lick their own furry balls. Disgusting creatures. They should all be muzzled— and castrated."

"You witches are harsh! I'm sorry, but I just can't resist those puppy dog eyes." Isabel cooed.

I was shocked at the conversation playing out before me. "Wait! You're saying werewolves are real? What else? Fairies? Vampires?"

"Besides werewolves, it's just us old witches, sweetie, there hasn't been a vampire around in centuries. Enough of this silly talk. Now, back to your book. We've discussed this at some length and from now on we want you to consider us your creative editors, so to speak." Hilda explained.

"Well, I—I don't know, really. I just started this and to tell the truth, I am doing nothing more than dabbling with writing a story."

"Oh, dear! No, don't sell yourself short. You've got it. We just want to help out once in a while. Maybe provide you with some plot ideas. Rest assured, we know what makes a good story and let's just say, it is highly advisable that you consider our suggestions. In fact, we insist you continue writing your paranormal romance. You can back out, but only if you can find another witch that has the power to use the desk." Isabel tauntingly smiled.

I knew right then the reason why the desk was given away for free by the odd old woman. She must have thrown in the towel. Before I could make any decision about it, I had some questions. I was still thinking that if I could get a grip on this magic, I could really do some great things for people, as well as have some fun with writing. "Excuse me, but is there any way I can get some training for my new witchcraft power? I would really like to get a grasp on what it is that I should or shouldn't do. I've had a few—incidents, you could say."

Isabel answered, "Oh yes, of course. I almost forgot! Your training program. We are sending a witch to spend a little time with you. She will be able to help you hone your magic and answer all of your questions. So consider yourself an apprentice right now, and no magic unless it is approved by your new mentor."

Esmeralda snickered in the background. I was a little unsure why she did it. It left me with an unsettled feeling that things weren't quite right. To make things worse, the other witches had sly smiles plastered to their faces. I had to tell myself—that's just how witches are. Of course, if you really think about it, when you refer to someone as a witch, it generally isn't a compliment.

The witches each added their parting comments as they surprisingly ended our meeting a little earlier than I expected.

Hilda was the first one who started to shoo me out of the door. "Now, please pay Esmeralda your dues on the way out."

"No more willy-nilly magic spells off the internet," Marie added.

Isabel wanted just one thing, her werewolf. "Just concentrate on a delicious werewolf story for me, doll! Mama needs some alpha male!"

"Okay. I guess it would be good to have somebody show me the ropes. Now, how exactly do I get home? And please don't tell me by riding a broom. I have no desire to go rocketing through the sky with nothing between my ass and the earth but a cheap Dollar Store broom. That's another thing. Why the broom? Why not fly on something a little more comfortable? Maybe a recliner?" With that little slip of sarcasm, I had triggered a telling response from the witches. Their shocked expressions were so apparent, you would think they had just witnessed an alien tap dance across the floor.

Surprisingly, Marie scolded me. Her voodoo priestess accent made it seem more of an ominous warning. "Leigh, you are now a young witch. Please don't carelessly disrespect one of our most cherished symbols. The broom is a timeless and honored reminder of our past. Karma is a bitch, and it appears from your recent spell-crafting, *that* wicked bitch has *you* on her radar. So choose your words carefully."

Isabel called back to Esmeralda, "Dear, would you take care of Leigh's dues and arrange for her and Luna to get back home?"

"Of course. Come on, Leigh. There is someone in the lobby already waiting for you."

Chapter Two
Meet Gertie O'Leary

Esmeralda led me back through the doors into the reception area. A woman about my age stood at the desk. She was very thin and had reddish blonde hair that curled down onto the shoulders of a cute flowered summer dress. When she gave me a genuine bright smile, I thought she looked so perfectly little, cute, and most importantly, completely harmless. She looked nothing like a stereo typical witch. She didn't even look like the little black dress club that I had just met. "Hi, Leigh! I am so excited to meet you! I'm Gertie. Gertie O'Leary."

Now, I have to say this. We all know one or two bubbly people. You know, those friends that are always so cheerful you swear they consumed enough Prozac and fairy dust to make even the most terrible situation seem delightful. Those are the Bubblers. They just smile and giggle as they say things like, "Oh look, another speeding ticket! That's what I get for not being a more considerate driver," or "I just got fired from my job! Giggle—giggle. I'll finally have time to make cupcakes for everyone and bring them in to the lunchroom!" Or even, "Oh darn, they stopped making Twinkies, like forever! Giggle—giggle—I'm pretty sure I can come up with a super healthy alternative!"

No. No news was too devastating for the Bubblers. Sure sometimes they can be a little annoying, but I just love them. They balance out the world from all of the chronic whiners, drama queens, and bitches on the other side of the emotional personality pendulum. I consider myself one of those people right in the middle by the way, but we all have our days.

I reached out to shake her hand, and as I should have expected, she launched herself at me with outstretched arms. She was a hugger as well. Hugger Bubblers are a common combination, if you've noticed. "Hi, Gertie, I'm happy to meet you, too." I genuinely meant it. If I have to be a witch's understudy, Gertie would at least keep things fun. I wouldn't want any of those other snooty witches I had met. I knew right away that Gertie and I would get along just fine.

She took Luna from my arms and nuzzled her face into Luna's long black fur. "Meow, Meow." I cringed as I anticipated Luna's reaction, and then there was nothing but loud purring. The last person that had tried to stick their face into Luna's fur like that was Kelly. She ended up running through my house shrieking a blood curdling scream while Luna dug all four claw studded paws worth of pain into either side of her scalp. Luna looked like she was trying to wrestle a soccer ball. Luna had completely covered Kelly's face so that she couldn't see the chair that she tripped over as she darted around the room in terror. The real screaming, the screaming that got my neighbor to call the police, was when Luna broke free and ran off, two long locks of Kelly's hair streaming from her paws. Apparently, Luna loved something about Gertie. In general, the old grouch was really enjoying this witchcraft business. She really was like a new cat.

Gertie handed Luna back to me, and then looked at me with her hands on her hips and a smile on her face. "Now, I can't read minds like they do around this place. I suppose you're wondering why I'm not like the other witches here at the union. That's because they are all very old. Centuries old. I think it makes them a bit cranky. Me, I'm twenty-four years old and I age normally, just like you. Here's the thing, though, I was born in 1850, but then I was frozen in time in 1871. I was frozen for forty years! And then in 1911 I was freed, but it only lasted for another year until I was frozen in time again. That lasted one hundred years. So I've only been back for a couple of years now. I just don't count all of those frozen years towards my age. Can you blame me?"

"Hell no, Gertie. I'm in no hurry to hit one hundred." I was figuring out the math in my head when I began to worry about this whole frozen in time issue. "And you were frozen in time? Oh my God! Seriously? Who did that to you? Is that a normal thing?"

"Well, it seems that I had a little mishap—so, yeah, you could call it that, a mishap. The first time I was frozen it was because a certain witch became very upset with me—" Gertie paused and looked down at her feet before she finished speaking in a sad tone, "and she froze me in the arctic for forty years. I just skipped an entire forty years and didn't even know it. She wasn't a very nice person, not at all." Gertie instantly shrugged off her sad look and then smiled at me in true Hugger Bubbler fashion. "But that's all water under the bridge now! Here I am and none worse for the wear!"

Esmeralda wriggled her way into the conversation. "Mishap? Hah! Leigh, I'm certain you've heard of the Great Chicago Fire of 1871. Supposedly, it was started when Ms. O'Leary's cow kicked a lantern over." She bowed and waved her arm towards Gertie. "I now present to you, the one, the only, Ms. Gertrude O'Leary. The witch who singlehandedly burnt down the whole damn city of Chicago. Unfortunately, her cow was not able to be present today."

"Oh my God! Seriously? You? You're the infamous Ms. O'Leary?" I was really surprised. Gertie looked nervous and shaken. I knew this was a pretty painful memory for even a Hugger Bubbler to handle so I smiled at her and said, "Ah, well, that's ancient history. Isn't it? History has proven that if Chicago didn't burn down, it never would have been rebuilt into the modern metropolis it is today. So consider yourself a hero of sorts."

"Oh, Leigh, thanks for saying that. Really it was a mishap. I had just found a book on magic spells and I was trying them out. Who knew Latin could be such a tongue twister?" Gertie shrugged her shoulders and smiled nervously. "Well, I was trying to transform a little mouse into a cat. I just love cats, you know. Anyway, when I finished the spell, instead of a black and white cat that I hoped for, I had a large black and white cow bolting through the house. It knocked over the candles and started the curtains on fire."

"Wow! Well at least the old story rings true. The fire was caused by a cow."

"Not exactly. The cow ran out the back door. I immediately pulled down the flaming curtains and threw them out of the window. I didn't even think about where they would land. Who knew that the building next door was packed to the rafters with dry goods? Not me, obviously. Well, those curtains went out my window and right into an open window of that old building. The next thing I see is a giant bonfire blazing away outside. So, it wasn't exactly the poor cow's fault. That place was a firetrap really."

'Oh, of course, that was a complete accident, Gertie. I can totally relate." I looked over at Esmeralda who had her arms folded across her chest and her head tilted to the side. She looked at me in complete disbelief. It was true, I could relate, considering how my summer break had gone so far.

"Leigh, why don't you ask Gertie what happened *after* she thawed out? I'm pretty sure she remembers what happened. After all, another pissed off witch froze her for one hundred years."

Gertie's eyes bugged out as she mouthed the words. "No, please!"

"No, Esmeralda. I really don't care." Of course, I was dying to know, but I didn't want to give Esmeralda the satisfaction of listening to a confession from Gertie. That was pretty cruel of Esmeralda. "I'm sure if Gertie ever feels like telling me about it, she will." Once I said that, Esmeralda huffed and went back behind her reception desk. She turned on a radio to some obscure 1970's music program.

Gertie let out the breath she must have been holding. "Oh thank you, Leigh! That was so nice of you to get her off that topic. I promise I'll tell you all about those unfortunate things later. I'll be visiting you soon, I hope you don't mind. I have to finish a few things here and then I should stop by for a visit next week. I'm especially excited to read some of your books. I've never met a writer before!"

"Well, don't get too excited Gertie, you haven't met one yet. I'm really an elementary teacher. The writing is more like a hobby. And as it turns out, my hobby has me heading to the twilight zone with stops at the looney bin along the way. It will be nice to spend some time together, though. I'm glad I'm not in this alone, and I just know I can learn a lot from you. Oh, and feel free to stop by whenever you like! Just one question. Were the witches in the boardroom the ones that froze you?"

"Oh no! Not them, although those old witches all know each other. They kind of run the witches union like it's their club, or something like that. They want to stick their noses into everything. They can be pretty forceful in getting their way. I find it is best to just avoid them. Now—"

"Wait. Like a club? Or more like the mob?"

"Mob? You mean like a big angry mob?"

"No. No, Gertie, I mean like a group of criminals."

"Shh, don't say those things, Leigh! Not here. We can talk about it next week. Don't worry about them right now. So—let's get you and Luna home! First, you are missing the one item that every witch needs, a broom." Gertie dug around in a large tote that hung over her shoulder. When I say large, I mean beach bag size. By the looks of the huge silk blossoms sewn on to it, the girl sure loved flowers.

Gertie squealed in a pitch above her normally high voice. "Here! I found it! I feel so honored to be the one to present you with your first official witches broom!" She retrieved a tiny little broom that actually looked like a paintbrush.

"Um, really? I'm almost afraid to ask how I'm going to fly on that thing."

"It's more of a symbol I guess you could say. But it is really magic and very important for a witch to have. I feel like we should perhaps be doing some sort of solemn ceremony. It just seems like such an important thing. What do you say, Leigh?"

Esmeralda groaned in response to Gertie's suggestion. I really wanted to be on my way so I countered with an alternate plan. One that wouldn't include Esmeralda's snickering observations. "How about we do that when you come visit? That way it will be just you, Luna, and me."

"Oh! That would be great! We'll have fun. We can even dress up! But you will have to take your broom with you for now so you can get home." Gertie stood back a little to teach me the spell. In the background Esmeralda's radio was droning with the *Soothing Sounds of the Seventies* radio show. An acoustic guitar ballad caught Gertie's perky little ears for a minute. "Oh, what a beautiful song about the Rocky Mountains! I have so much music to catch up on. Oh well. Now, let's get you guys back home. To be instantly transported to anywhere you want to go, you just do this. First, you have to stand perfectly still and hold the broom in one hand. Then, you just say the magic words.

Witch's flight, day or night

To and fro, take me now to where I must go."

Gertie stopped short of finishing the spell to comment on the song that was still playing. "Oh, this is the best part of the song." Gertie sang out part of the chorus. "Rocky Mountain High, Colorado." She smiled at me, and then continued on with her lesson. "Anyway, then you just say the place you need to go to. Easy!"

I stood nice and straight. With Luna in one hand and the little broom in the other, I repeated the phrase.

"Witch's flight, day or night

To and Fro, take me now where I must go."

I can never miss an opportunity to have a little fun, so I mimicked Gertie's impromptu karaoke performance. I sang out, "Rocky Mountain High, Colorado." I chuckled and looked at Gertie. "Sorry, I just couldn't resist!"

"Oh, that was pretty funny and pretty good, too!" She paused and then a startled look appeared on her face. "Wait! You were supposed to say where you have to go!"

"Oh, I was getting to that. Now, take me to—" Then I was suddenly lost in a puff of colored smoke.

Chapter Three
Rocky Mountain High

"Denver? Fucking Denver? As in Denver fucking Colorado?" My eyes anxiously darted around the city street before me. A police car was parked across the street and I saw the logo on the door. It clearly read: City of Denver Police Department. I saw a business address stenciled on the glass door of an office building near me. The address read: Denver, Colorado. "What the hell is going on? How did I know I was actually casting the spell!" I shouted. Only a couple of people on the busy sidewalk even gave me so much as a glance.

In a city you can get away with acting like a raving fool and nobody will bat an eyelash. There is always someone on the street howling out obscenities, paranoid statements, or predictions about the coming apocalypse. There I stood, holding up my little Barbie sized broom, yelling the F word and shouting nonsense about casting spells. To the pedestrian traffic I was just another bat-shit-crazy woman with a cat. Better not get involved. Just keep walking and pretend not to notice her and maybe she'll leave you alone.

"Damn! Seriously?" I stood on a street I didn't even know the name of, in a city I had never been to. With a cat. I guess this was exactly what the old voodoo witch meant about Karma biting me in the ass. I was confronted with a decision. I wondered if I should repeat the magic spell that Gertie taught me. At that point I was so stressed out, I wasn't certain if I would remember a word of it. I was more than a little frightened of where I could end up if something went wrong for a second time. The first thing was to just make a phone call. *Take that, Karma!* Those bitches hadn't been thinking 21st century. I'm a girl with a smartphone, I'm damn near invincible to Karma. With the touch of my fingers, I could book a flight faster than a jackrabbit on a hot date.

Then rotten news brought my hopes down. Due to dense fog in Chicago, all flights to my hometown were held in limbo. The schedule had gotten so bad that they simply cancelled any later fights. I was hopelessly stranded until my new flight late the next morning. Time for smartphone app number two. I would just get a hotel room. In less than ten minutes I had booked a room at a decent hotel near the airport, and best of all, they accepted one small pet.

I saw a line of taxis conveniently waiting on the corner at the end of the block. I placed Luna in my tote and I walked in their direction. Just as I passed by a small bakery along the way, I realized I hadn't eaten a thing all day. I turned around and dodged into the open door, or rather, I was pulled in by the aroma of fresh baked pastries. What I really craved was fresh baked brownies. I frantically scanned the display cases and saw a selection of baked goods that made my mouth water, but no brownies. I turned around to ask someone if, by chance, they had any in the back. What I saw made me freeze. There on the counter by the register was a clear, cling-wrapped paper plate with four of the biggest, most delicious looking brownies I had ever seen. I had to make them mine. I walked up to a young red haired guy at the register. From the looks of his t-shirt, long matted dread locks, which I think he should just call red locks, scruffy whiskers, and a brightly colored knit cap, he had to be Bob Marley's biggest fan in Denver. To top it off, he was wearing what appeared to be a kilt. A frayed and dingy looking gray flannel kilt. The huge, scrumptious brownies were on the counter close to him. I thought perhaps he must have wrapped up the last of them to keep for himself. I figured that if I would joke around a little with him, maybe he would sell at least one brownie to me. "Hi! Those are my brownies right there. I'm here for them. Come to mama!"

"Yeah? Well, now to whom may I ask placed this special order?" The scruffy hippie looked at me with red, watery eyes.

"Um, Leigh?" I was surprised that he wanted to know my name. We don't do that in Chicago.

"Right on, Lee." He pushed the pack of brownies across the counter to me. Luna poked her head out of my tote and called out a hungry "Meow".

I nudged and dug around Luna for some cash and asked, "How much do I owe you?"

"Naw, it's all good. It's all paid up. Lee is cool." He said and went back to reading his book.

"Huh? I'm not sure I understand." I couldn't believe he would just give them to me because he liked my name. Clearly one of us was confused and from the looks of him, it certainly wasn't me.

"Yeah, I already got the cash. Lee is good. It's cool." He began to look a little puzzled and then shook his head before turning back to his book.

What the fuck is up with this guy? I thought to myself. I curbed my Chicago tongue and decided I had best use my manners. "Well, thank you. It just seemed a little odd." I wasn't about to argue with the guy. These were the last brownies in the bakery and since they were free, it made them that much better.

The Celtic Bob Marley looked up from his book. "Hey, what's wrong with you? Are you a cop or something?"

"Huh? What's wrong with me? You've got some chutzpah asking me that! Looking like you do. Maybe I should be asking what's wrong with you, MacMarley! Besides, why would a cop be carrying a cat in her purse and looking for brownies?" I shook my head in disbelief, picked up the large package of brownies, and started to walk out. I turned around and threw a five dollar bill on the counter because I didn't want him to run out and accuse me of shoplifting the baked goods. With that, I spun around and headed back onto the busy sidewalk. "Damn pothead or something." I mumbled.

I was pretty sure I heard him mumble something as well. "Damn stoners."

What a weirdo! What's wrong with me? That's a laugh coming from him. I suppose I am not really as offended as I am just plain disappointed. I finally get to see a real live guy in a kilt and instead of him being a hot hunk of Scottish manhood, he is a scrawny rat-boy that lives in a dumpster. Not that I want to meet another guy. I'm just curious about this whole kilt thing. Kelly had been drooling over hot Scots in kilts ever since she started reading that romance series. She makes them out to be so hot. And why is he asking if I was a cop? Weird guy, I suppose weird questions should be expected.

There was one thing that had been nagging me ever since I tried to book a room. What the hell was I going to do without a litter box for Luna? Eventually this was going to become an issue, and I had to figure out a solution before my purse became a kitty port-a-potty. My next stop was a convenience store that was quite—

convenient as well. With the purchase of a small bag of cat litter, an aluminum foil roasting pan, some cans of cat food, and some snacks for me, I had solved that little problem.

I spotted a yellow cab on the corner and hurried along the sidewalk to catch it. I'm convinced taxis around the country are required to use the same incense laced air fresheners. It's nothing you would be able to find in any auto parts store. It's an odd combination of sandalwood, citrus, and the lingering smell of onions. As long as I'm on the topic of air fresheners, we all know they don't really freshen anything. They normally mix with whatever putrid smell is hanging in the air, creating a whole new horrid scent. The bathrooms in gas stations that spray a cloud of citrus down upon the latest guest always leaves a new combination scent for the next visitor. And there is nothing quite like the disgusting smell of shitrus.

I told the driver the name of the hotel that I had made reservations at, and we were on our way. I reached down and unwrapped the first brownie. Luna had been sitting in my bag with her head sticking out one side and her tail hanging out of the other. She looked at the brownie and then at me. Her big eyes were pleading for something to eat and then she began to cry. It was pretty effective, too. I broke a decent chunk of the brownie off and gave it to her. She quickly took the tasty treat and disappeared into the depths of the bag. All I could think about was eating the brownie, I didn't even care that I would have an excuse to go purse shopping. I imagined it would look pretty bad after Luna made use of it as her personal food dish.

Now, I have heard so many women scolding their men about wolfing down food, just as most women try to never publicly display the scene that unfolded next. It was that natural phenomenon. The fact is, if you leave a hungry girl alone with a giant, fresh baked piece of heaven, she will descend on it like a school of piranhas devouring an unfortunate bathing cow in a furious maelstrom of fins, tails, and blood. In no time I was licking the sweet chocolate remains from my fingers. I thought, *why stop there?* I grabbed another brownie and wolfed it down. It was an extreme move, but really, we've all done it before.

I arrived at the hotel and quickly checked in. I set my bag on the bed and opened it, but nothing happened. I was very surprised that Luna hadn't sprung out, as I expected her to. I peered into my bag and there she was, curled up and purring. I thought it would be a good idea to make sure she had her box ready, so I set up the little foil pan and filled it with litter. I picked her up and laid her limp body on the bed. She rolled onto her back and made several very slow swatting motions with her paws. I was trying to comprehend what she was doing and I suddenly realized I had been staring at her for what seemed like hours.

I looked at my watch and saw I had only been in my room for a few minutes. The whole world had slowed down. I began to feel dizzy, or at least something similar to feeling dizzy, and a little sick to my stomach. The inside of my mouth felt like it had been salted and dried in the desert sun. All at once it felt like my brain had decided to start playing hopscotch. Things just didn't make sense. I was having some sort of psychotic break that I had never experienced before. The next feeling that came over me was hunger. This was the kind of hunger that must be what starvation feels like. The rest of the brownies cured my cravings.

Then it was if time stood still. I was really worried that this was another witchcraft problem. I was utterly convinced I was going to be in that state for the rest of my life. I felt nervous, but at the same time I was shifting into an odd euphoria. I felt so strange. I decided lying down on the bed would be my best bet for survival. I laid there staring at the textured pattern on the ceiling. I remembered watching a news story about bedbug infestations at hotels. I started to scratch myself. I could feel them! I believed that an invisible plague of tiny bedbugs had swarmed over my entire body. They were drilling into my skin! I could picture it. Dead certain I saw a construction crew of little bugs jackhammering into my leg, I swatted at them. Luna laid next to me and continued to swat at something in the air. Fireflies!

I rolled onto the floor to escape the bedbug army. To add to the strangeness, the clock radio came off the nightstand when I crashed on to the floor. The radio began to play a classic rock song. Apparently I'm cursed by random oldies for my personal soundtrack. The song was the 1970's hit, *Dust in The Wind.* If you've never heard the lyrics, all you need to know is it is probably the biggest buzzkill song ever written. It answers the question pondered by history's greatest philosophers. What happens to us when we die? What are we really? And according to this song the answer is: "All we are is dust in the wind."

The lyrics soaked into my mind and I then realized I had died. This was the end. This is what it meant to be dead. I had a very anxious moment when I thought about how I felt like I was the only person that existed on some strange planet, and I was dead. It was like my soul had been ripped out of me and then pulled over me like a blanket. I was just contemplating the origin of blankets and who invented them when I looked up and saw the phone on the edge of the nightstand. I pulled it down and read the little label under the keypad. Dial 0 for Front Desk. I looked at Luna and said, "Seriously? That's what they call it? Well played, God! Front Desk. I like that." I decided I had to dial zero for the front desk and let them know they had another dead person checked in and waiting.

"Front Desk, Jesus speaking." This of course was the Spanish given name pronounced *hay-zeus*.

"Ahh, Jesus. I get it! Nice idea to use the Spanish version of your name. So, the Christians had it right all along?"

"Excuse me?"

"I hope it's okay. I didn't mean any offense. I was raised Jewish, and there isn't a whole lot you can do about that is there? Well, I mean except in your case. Your honor." I started giggling uncontrollably.

"Is there anything I can do for you, ma'am?"

"Yes, well, I am just calling to let you know I understand now. I'm dead. It's fine. I get it, so go ahead and teleport me or whatever you do next."

"Ma'am, I've got a lot of other guests to take care of here tonight. If you don't mind, please don't bother me with your problems."

"Oh, what happened? Plane crash? You know I was going to take a plane today. Did I take a plane that actually crashed and that's how I died? And I just think I got a hotel room?"

"Listen lady. I am getting pretty sick of all of you tourists that come here to sample the latest strains. Now go to sleep or whatever, but don't call me anymore. Damn legalization." The loud smack told me he had slammed the receiver down and ended the call.

Luna rolled off the bed and landed on top of me. "Oh my God! Oh my God! I just pissed off Jesus and he hung up on me! I have to call someone. I wonder if I can contact the living." I actually waited for Luna to respond, but she just stared at me with her eyes wide open.

Chapter Four
Phone Call from Beyond

I got up and grabbed my phone from the tote. Who should I call once I find out I'm dead? Or should I just text them? I was perplexed at my contacts list and realized I should have a separate list of who to call when I'm dead. These are the sort of things that one should take care of while still alive, like life insurance. I looked through the names and saw my parents' number. "Oh God, no! I can't handle my mother, right now." Then I saw Hunter's number. "Aww, Hunter. I am going to really miss him. I never even had the chance to have sex with him."

"Meow."

"You think I should call him?"

"Meow. Meow."

Panic was again coming over me, and I seemed to be struggling to keep from being dragged down in an undertow from a giant wave of insanity. I held onto Luna and kissed the top of her head. "I'm sorry, I got us killed. Don't you have at least one of your nine lives left?"

I looked at Hunter's contact number glowing on my phone. I had to exert actual physical force to get my finger to make the call.

"Hey, Leigh! How are you doing? What's up?"

"Hi, Hunter. I have some bad news, I'm dead."

"What? What are you talking about?"

"Yep. Dead. I think it was a plane crash. Now everything is weird. Time is standing completely still here, wherever I am. Oh, and I pissed off Jesus something fierce."

"Leigh! Listen, I don't know what's wrong. Are you drunk or something? Did you hit your head?"

"Of course not! I told you that I'm dead, and I'm in Denver of all places. Oh, and Luna is with me."

"Luna? Denver? As in Denver, Colorado? What the hell?"

"Yep! That's the place you go to. Who would have thought? What really sucks is I never got to have sex with you before I died. I was really looking forward to that."

"Listen, Leigh, I need to ask you something. Is there any special medication you may have forgotten to take today?"

"Nooooooo, I don't think so."

"Okay. Good. Now, what did you have to eat or drink today?"

"Water and a little nibble of a brownie." I lied my ass off because I pictured myself wolfing down those brownies in the taxi. I just didn't want to share that image with Hunter.

"Well, I can't imagine anything happening from that." There was nothing but silence and then Hunter came up with a possibility. "You said a brownie. Where exactly did you get that brownie?"

"Just a bakery. Bob MacMarley was trying to hog them for himself, but he ended up giving them to me. It was really weird." I was struggling to focus on Hunter's question. "Kilts. I just don't get kilts. You don't wear a kilt, do you?"

"Um, no, I've never even gave it a thought. Why?"

"I have no idea, but I'm starving now." I reached into the bag of snacks I picked up. I knew I wanted to have something a little bit healthier than brownies, so I grabbed some of the honey granola and some trail mix. With the trail mix, you can fool people into thinking you're eating something healthy, but you are really just picking out the chocolate. I started munching on the granola like I was a squirrel that stuffs its face with seeds. "Hmmph," I tried to continue speaking as bits of granola peppered the phone.

"Anyway, Leigh, I think I know what that brownie was. Marijuana is legal there and they sell certain foods that are loaded with it. It doesn't make much sense that you could have gotten one of those, though. I'm pretty sure you would have had to go into a special store and showed your ID. I mean, you would have known what it was. What about that bakery you went to? You said the guy just gave some brownies to you?"

"Um Hm, crunch, crunch, crunch. Fo Fee."

"My guess is that he gave you some pot brownies. That guy was probably selling them without going through whatever legal system they have. You know, selling them illegally. You probably ate more than you realize."

I washed down the granola with a warm soda. "Hell, I ate all four! They were good, too! Even Luna had a little." Oops.

Hunter was clearly tapping away on his computer and laughing. "Leigh, you have all the symptoms of a pot overdose! I just looked it up. And those brownies were probably meant for a whole group of people. You've had something like sixteen or even twenty times the normal amount meant for one person! Jesus!"

"Oh, Jesus, you can catch him by dialing zero from my room. I wouldn't bother him now. He seems really busy and irritated. Wait, what did you just say about those brownies? Seriously! So, I'm not dead! Wow! Now I know why MacMarley said they were already paid for.

He thought I was someone else that had been sent to pick up the brownies."

"From everything I've read here, it is harmless. Your brain is just flipping out. The best thing you can do is just go to sleep. I also read that the effects from edible marijuana products could last several hours. Try not to think too much."

"This has just been one hell of a day. I think you're right, I need to sleep. I'm afraid to though. My head feels like it is buzzing. I'll never fall asleep, though. I'll just lay in a fetal position and worry about things like garden gnomes. And the fact that I can add drug mule to my résumé."

"Okay. Well, how about we just talk? I won't make you think too hard. You tell me whatever comes to mind and I'll listen. If you want to ask me anything, go ahead."

"I would absolutely love that. I wish you were here, though." Something very naughty crossed my mind. Or I should say it came into my mind, looked around, and vanished. I absentmindedly grabbed for more granola. I damn near broke my teeth on it. "Pleth!" I sprayed out the granola. "What the hell! This isn't granola! Its trail mix and it tastes like absolute shit. Yuck. And it's like pieces of rock!" I looked at the handful and my brain told me I should pick out the chocolate, but all I had was dry little chunks of granola. "It smells like my mom's perfume!"

"Leigh! Wait. Double check what you're eating."

"Oh. My. God." I was shocked at what I had done. I looked at the bag of trail mix and saw I hadn't opened it. I had just scooped up a handful of kitty litter out of the bag. I had actually tried to eat kitty litter! Thank God I hadn't gotten a handful out of the litter box. Before I could wonder if perhaps that is what I had actually done,

Hunter started laughing at the situation and that got me laughing about it.

"So, tell me more about how you were looking forward to having sex with me."

"Oh, God! Can you read minds, too?"

Hunter let the sex conversation pass by and we talked for almost two hours. I told him about every scatterbrained thing that came to mind, and he told me about his family and all of the places he had traveled to. I was so grateful to have someone to talk to. I was finding out more and more about Hunter. I was relieved he wasn't just another hottie that sported a false persona just to get a girl interested. You know the type of guy I'm talking about. They make you feel like the people on those TV shows about antiques. Some young woman happily unveils her newfound prize only to find out it is not only worthless, but an intentional fake. Surprise! That Mr. Right you just found is actually a full time social work project. So far Hunter seemed genuine. Who else would be willing to listen to some rambling nonsense from a girl barely hanging on to reality?

At some point in our conversation I had to cough up some sort of explanation for my unplanned stay in Denver. Hunter had never questioned me, but I knew it was an odd situation that would just have to make him wonder about me. As the effects of the brownies dissipated, I was able to come up with a plausible reason for my quick trip to Colorado. I told him I had signed up for a one day education conference in Denver.

Being deceitful to Hunter made me feel like crap, but I don't think I had much of a choice. If I would have brought up magic and the witches union, he would think it wasn't just the brownies messing me up. I might as well show up at his police academy graduation in a straightjacket. In the end I can say I really loved talking to him, even though my brain didn't always join in. Finally, I felt extremely sleepy and we said our goodbyes. That night Luna curled up and slept on top of me. She had never done that before.

I laid in the bed and wondered about the witches union. I was more than a little worried about what I could have possibly gotten myself mixed up in, especially since they made a point to tell me that they would be making certain suggestions for the story I started to write. I became convinced they had something much larger than a good story planned. Maybe it was time to step away from the witchcraft, but I knew somehow that wasn't going to be an option.

Chapter Five
Aftermath

When I woke up, I immediately had a sense of dread about facing Hunter. I had zero experience with marijuana, and even if I had, it wouldn't have prepared me for ingesting enough of it to stone my entire neighborhood. I remembered everything, although parts of it seemed more like I had dreamt it. My idea to call Hunter was a remarkably bad decision, even for me. Okay, it was downright stupid. I just wanted to be home, in my own bed. At least I wasn't dealing with a hangover, so that was a huge plus.

I sat with my head in my hands and hoped I could find a way to just forget that any of it had ever happened. There were a few times I actually found myself speaking out loud. "Hunter! Ugh!" Finally I found a way to deal with it. And it wasn't by memorizing a viral Facebook meme. That morning was not a time for that kind of talk. No, you can just disregard all of those little tidbits of advice you hear about facing your issues and dealing with your problems. I am referring to those positive little memes that the Bubblers post all over Facebook. They sound really good and they are often quotes by someone you feel like everyone knows, except you. So you google them, like I sometimes do.

Sometimes optimism and positivity are best applied to other things, like diets or stress reduction. You know those little resolutions you've already subconsciously decided that there is a 95% chance they will fail anyway. I have no appetite for having to deal with an issue that reminds you that you've made a complete ass of yourself in front of the one person you want to impress the most. The only choice for you is to try to not think about it, ever. Bury the seething memory away, like you are hiding a body. If it should be brought up, go to the most extreme measures to change the topic, even if it requires you drop to the ground and fake a case of acute appendicitis.

Surprisingly, my trip home was uneventful. As I considered how things had been going lately, I was mentally prepared for a complete disaster. When the taxi dropped me off in front of my apartment, I don't think I had ever been happier to finally be home, and for an elementary school teacher, that says a lot.

I let Luna loose so she could sneak from room to room, as if she thought it was too good to be true. I was pretty sure that after the trip she was just on, she didn't trust her senses one bit. "It's okay, Luna kitty. We're really home now. And I promise no more magic spells or magic brownies." Luna arched her back and made an ugly hiss at me before she disappeared into the shadows. "Damn it, one step forward and two steps back with you. You were finally starting to act like a regular cat instead of a damn wild opossum, or raccoon, or—whatever. Ungrateful bitch!" Of course, she really did have a reason to be mad. After all, I did whisk her thousands of miles away, drug her, take her to a hotel, and make her use a foil turkey roasting pan for a toilet.

All I really wanted to do at that point was find something to eat, soak in a bath, and then crawl in to bed. As usual, by the time I got one toe in the bath, my doorbell rang. Wrapped in a towel, I gingerly tiptoed to the door and looked out of my peephole, only to see a close-up eyeball. "Leigh! Leigh! Open up. I know your looking out of that little hole right now!" Kelly, of course. I reluctantly opened the door.

"Kelly! And what a surprise, it's also Lindsey!" So much for a quiet bath.

"Where the hell have you been?" Kelly was more pissed than concerned.

"You left us with super stalkers!" Lindsey was visibly shaken.

"Sorry! Really, I was on my way over there when I was summoned to appear before the officers of the Witches Union."

"Huh? What? Are you on drugs or something?" Kelly went from angry to puzzled.

Did she know something? How? Hunter? No way. She's just being a smartass. "No! Of course not! You know I have absolutely no interest in even trying drugs. And for the record, I do want to say that I am in line with the latest poll numbers, marijuana should not be classified as a drug."

"Wait, why did she just answer your rhetorical smartass statement, Kelly? You don't think she is really—you know—using?"

Kelly crossed her arms and looked smugly at Lindsey. "Oh! You're right, Lindsey! Why would she say that? Normally she just ignores my snide remarks. It's so obvious. Because Leigh has just let on that she has a little secret to share! Isn't that right, Leigh?" Kelly had turned to me and was tapping her foot. A knowing smirk covered her face. She might as well have just shouted out "Gotcha." My phone started to ring, but it was in my bedroom, so I just let it go. I figured it was my weekly call from my parents, and I really didn't want to add any more craziness to the day. "Shouldn't you get that call, Leigh?"

"No, it's probably just my parents."

"Probably your dealer!" Kelly was kidding with me, but I knew she had already gotten some genuinely worried looks from Lindsey, and she had every intention of playing this up for her own amusement.

"No! For God sakes, Kelly! And there really is a Witches Union. And they ordered me to appear before them. And I flew home on my broom." I reached into my purse that was sitting on an end table by the door. I pulled out the little miniature witches broom and held it up. "See? This is what I can instantly travel with!"

"Oh my God!" Lindsey squeaked out. "Is that one of those crack thingies? Oh, Leigh! You poor girl." Tears started to run down her face. "If we would only have known you had become a—a junkie, or cracker, or whatever they call them." She ran up and hugged me.

Kelly looked at Lindsey in complete disbelief. "Lindsey. Seriously. A crack thingy? And did you just call her a cracker?"

"How the hell would I know about all this druggie stuff? I grew up in East Krok, Wisconsin, population twelve."

At this point, Kelly was laughing so hard she was making her little snorting noise.

I pushed Lindsey off of me. "No! Just listen, and I'll tell you exactly what happened." I recalled the entire ordeal from start to finish.

"Okay, Leigh, you know the agreement. Hand over Hunter's number to us. He is going to be fair game."

"What are you talking about, Kelly? What agreement?" I was caught completely off guard.

"I'd say that there is a 99.9% chance Hunter has already deleted you from his phone contacts and has you pegged as a first class nut job. If you recall the agreement, if any one of us has dibs on a guy and it doesn't work out, he then becomes fair game for us. Provided, of course, that the first interested party, namely *you*, has not had sex with said hunky male. In that case, all best friends will shun any contact with him. And since you haven't hooked up with Hunter before screwing it up, we deserve to get a shot at him."

Lindsey was now excited and wide eyed. "Oh! That's right, Kelly! Hand over the keys, Leigh. Time to let someone else take the wheel."

"First of all, Hunter seemed genuinely concerned with my well-being, and he is a great listener. Unlike you two. Secondly, aren't you both currently dealing with super stalkers?" I had to admit to myself I had been very worried about how it was going to go with Hunter. We hadn't set up any more dates and I was quite concerned, to say the very least.

Just then there was a purple and pink puff of smoke in my living room. It was accompanied by a loud noise, like the cracking of a whip. The smoke cleared and there stood Gertie dressed in her apparent trademark look. A brightly colored floral print sleeveless dress and a large floppy sun hat.

Gertie was in the middle of belting out an eighties classic, and she sang at the top of her lungs. "Pour some sugar on me!"

"Jesus in a jukebox!" Kelly yelled.

"What the fu–" Lindsey managed to squeak out before she fainted.

I immediately assessed the situation that had so suddenly made a three ring circus appear in my tiny living room.

Ladies and Gentlemen! Under the big top for today only! The Sunshine Girl will appear out of thin air and entertain you in song! The Amazing Frazzled Woman will be wearing nothing but a faded Hello Kitty towel as she performs a complete mental breakdown before your very eyes! Spectators so shocked they will be fainting and speaking in tongues! All I could manage to say out loud was, "God, help me."

We all ran to her and she quickly recovered. I held Lindsey's head up. "Gertie, meet my best friends, Kelly and Lindsey. Sorry. Up to this point the only magic they've seen is the aftermath from using my magic desk. And—it seems like you've discovered eighties music."

"Oh yes! I love the eighties! Such catchy tunes! Nice to meet you girls!" Gertie bubbled with glee. Then she sang once more. "Like a virgin—"

"Are you one of those witches from the union?" Asked Kelly.

I jumped in and answered her question. "No, I'm sorry, I should have explained. Gertie was appointed by the Witches Union to give me some training. You know, so I hopefully won't repeat something like the grocery store explosion, or my sister's visit to the ER. She is going to be my mentor." Both Kelly and Lindsey had their faces contorted in expressions that pretty much just came out and said: *Her? You have got to be kidding me!*

"What?" I demanded an answer. "I can tell by your faces that either you don't think she is qualified or that I couldn't learn from her. Just go ahead and say what's on your minds."

"Oh no, it's not that at all, Leigh. It's just that she doesn't look like a real witch at all. I mean, I get it that you have sort of stumbled into the profession and you don't have the look. You know, *the look*. Long pointy nose with a pointy hat to match, green skin, black dress, broom, and all that jazz."

Kelly agreed. "Yeah. Shouldn't she be out in front of a grocery store, selling cookies? She sure doesn't look like a witch."

"Hey! You guys are stereotyping! Gertie is—"

Gertie interrupted me with a laugh, an uneasy little one. "It's fine, Leigh, really. Heck, I don't even think I look like a witch. Then again, I really haven't met a witch *yet* that does!" Then she looked a little less bubbly. I was pretty sure my friends had hurt her feelings and now she felt a little rejected.

Before I could demand an apology, both Kelly and Lindsey had noticed the saddened look on Gertie's face. Suddenly, they began falling over themselves to apologize and welcome her. Before long we were good. One circle of best friends that just got a little bigger by one.

"Well, why don't we all have a seat, and you guys can explain what is going on with you. The pair of hot and obsessed roofers, I assume? Maybe Gertie can help."

"Well, I only dropped by to see if you were doing well, Leigh. When you disappeared from the union lobby, I had no idea where in the world you ended up. But tell me more about these roofers. Hot and obsessed roofers, now that sounds—deliciously intriguing." Gertie blushed after she said that.

"Yep. Roofers, these guys were repairing Lindsey's leaky roof and I sort of cast a spell on two of them. More to the point, I made them absolutely devoted to Lindsey and Kelly. They can't think of anything or anyone else."

"Wow! Good one, Leigh! You know from what I've learned so far, very few witches are able to control someone so completely. The fact you were successful must have made the old witches on the union board go crazy with envy. Anyway, it's been going on too long now, so there isn't any chance of reversing the spell. It has to still be pretty fresh for that. I did run across a spell that can make someone ignore you."

"Kind of like an anti-stalker spell?" Kelly asked.

"I suppose you could say that. I'm not too sure we should use it. It's completely untried. And I have to be getting back to my pussies, now that I know you made it home in one piece."

"Your pussies?" I am pretty sure we all asked simultaneously.

"Yes. I have a lot of pussycats."

There was a collective sigh of relief and laughter was building up. "How many—pussycats would you say is a lot, Gertie?" I was really curious. Gertie didn't look like the crazy cat type to me.

"Four hundred and thirty two. After I was unfrozen the last time, I knew I wanted to do something really useful. I just love animals, especially cats. Well, I started my own shelter. A little bit of magic and I got my hands on an old farm in Louisiana. I call it the Pussy Plantation. I even designed my own signs so folks could find it. "

With that, we roared with laughter. I laughed so hard that I lost my towel.

"What? Why does everyone laugh at that?"

Kelly leaned over and whispered into Gertie's ear.

"Oh my God! I suppose it meant that same thing back in the old days, but it wasn't used very often. Not enough that people would have thought about *that* body part, just cats. That explains all of the truckers, bikers, and sailors that show up at all hours. I suppose I'll have to change the fliers that I hand out in New Orleans. I've been asking for donations to satisfy all of the pussies at the Pussy Plantation. Thank God I have a pack of really mean sounding dogs to chase them away before they set a foot on the farm!"

Now even Gertie was laughing with us. "I better be heading back home. Nothing worse than ignoring the pussies! It has been so nice to meet you ladies. I just know we are going to get along great!" She took out her little broom and with a few words and another puff of colorful mist, Gertie was headed back to her Louisiana pussy farm.

"Oh my God. She is a riot! I love her to pieces already." Lindsey said.

"Same here! Now, Leigh, fix our super stalker problem." Kelly looked at me with a hint of desperation in her eyes. "Please!"

Chapter Six
Taking matters into my own hands

I sure wished Gertie would have been able to stick around to help me out. I really had no idea how bad things could have been for Lindsey and Kelly. Really, how bad could it be to have a couple of hot guys worshipping you? Compared to my little jaunt through the rabbit hole via Denver, I figured they had it pretty damn good. I decided I would have to suck it up and see for myself, after I had a little time to get my head together.

I reassured Kelly and Lindsey, now that I was back home, I would think of something. It would just have to wait until after I stopped by and witnessed their behavior for myself. Peace and order were restored to my apartment, and I went back to getting into my bathtub for a long, well deserved soak. Normally, this was a time for me do some reading about Vlad's latest heroic exploits, not to mention his sexual prowess. Sadly, he was no more and to be honest, I don't think I really miss him all that much anymore. My bath was warm and overflowing with bubbles. I decided what I needed was to clear my head and think of nothing, but every time I closed my eyes, I was confronted by so many thorny images.

My summer break seemed to be slipping away already. There was the witches union that I was very unsure of. My friends were still stuck with a problem I created through magic, and I wasn't very happy that I had blown up my credit card on a needless stay in Denver. I thought about Gertie and she made me smile. I liked her. I tried not to think about Hunter, but it was impossible. I didn't want to start worrying about facing him and having to awkwardly discuss anything that had been said during our long phone call.

Still, the mere thought of his name brought about images of his smiling face and bright eyes. Those eyes, I loved them. Then of course, his muscular arms and that rock hard body were images that made me tingle. I remembered our trip to the mini-golf and how he held me from behind. I could still feel the warmth of his breath on my neck, just before I nearly cracked his skull and crushed his testicles. I immediately shook that thought out of my head and started thinking about how he again held me at the shooting gallery. We flirted and laughed. That touch of his! I was really getting warmed up thinking about him until I had the memory play out in my mind of the metal awning crashing down on his handsome head. I couldn't shake the embarrassment that made me want to disappear, and it only got worse when I thought about some of the things I said to him over the phone.

I sank myself down under the bubbles, as if I was hiding from myself. *Hunter.* His name was spoken slowly and sadly in my mind. I might as well just agree with Kelly and throw him to the girls. Just get it over with and watch as they fight over him like two dogs fighting over a bone. I popped up from the watery grave of my bath only to yell out loud, "Ugh! Hunter! Fuck, fuck, double fuck!"

Luna strolled into the bathroom, carrying something. "What is that? That better not be a goddamn mouse!" She dropped it.

"Meow. Meow."

"My phone?" She scooted my phone across the tile floor. Then I heard it. Just barely.

"Hello? Hello, Leigh? Are you there? Are you all right?"

"Hunter? Hunter! Oh my God!" I jumped out of the tub and nearly busted several bones trying to scramble to get my phone. For a few seconds I pondered how Luna could have answered an incoming call on my smartphone. *Perhaps her paws are compatible with the touchscreen.* I quickly wiped my hands on a towel and grabbed the phone.

"Hi, Hunter! I'm here, I'm fine."

"Whew! That was weird. I hadn't heard from you since you called from Denver. I called earlier, but didn't get an answer, and then when I called just now—it seemed like your cat answered. All I heard was her little cat noises. Then I heard you yelling my name and—well, you were yelling fuck over and over." Hunter chuckled and I grimaced.

"Oh, I was just relaxing in the bath and I slipped or something. Anyway, I'm sorry I missed your call earlier. Lindsey and Kelly stopped by, and when those two are around, it can be more than a little difficult to even answer a ringing phone."

"Oh, no big deal. Listen, I'm just glad to know you made it home, safe and sound."

When I heard him say those words, my heart skipped a few beats, and I was hoping he didn't hear me silently mouthing the words, "Oh, thank God!" Well, maybe it was completely silent. I was truly elated, because I knew then that Hunter hadn't written me off as a total lunatic. Not yet at least.

"Thank you! It really means a lot to me that you called."

"I actually have two more reasons to call you, Leigh. First of all, I would like nothing more than to take you out on a date again. This time we can skip that damn dangerous mini golf place, if you don't mind."

"Of course! I would love that. Just let me know when and I'll be ready. What was the second thing?"

"It's about your friends, Kelly and Lindsey. And the two guys on the roofing crew. I don't know what got into those boys' heads, but I'm getting a little worried. I can barely get ahold of them for work. When they do manage to show up, they spend most of their time texting or trying to call your friends. Those girls sure have made an impression on Luke and Derek. I honestly have never seen anything like it. It's almost as if they're under a spell or something!"

"Well, sometimes the right girl can be a little—bewitching." Yeah, I actually said that.

"Could you talk to Kelly and Lindsey? See if those guys are getting out of hand? I really wouldn't want them to get themselves in any kind of trouble. You know, restraining order kind of trouble."

"Oh, I'm sure that wouldn't happen, but I'll definitely talk to them about it. I'm sure they can straighten this all out." I bit my lip and wanted to just tell him to forget about it and get back to talking about our date. "So, any idea when you would like to get together? I'm pretty free." I tiptoed back to the bath and slid into the bubble filled tub.

"There's so much to do in the city. So many places that I haven't been to in years, but I would really like to check out."

The sound of Hunter's voice talking about taking me out was really a turn on. As he talked, I started just answering him with very short answers. "Uh hmm" and "Mmm," and of course, "Oh, yeah, uh hum." Not because I wasn't interested, but my mind was churning out some pretty naughty thoughts. I was debating on asking him what he would like to do to me if he were standing next to the bath. I sure as hell had a head full of smutty suggestions.

Sometime between him talking about going to the Field Museum and the Shedd Aquarium, one of my answers probably sounded a little more like, "Oh, yes!" If you know what I mean. Now that I was comfortable we were still good and moving forward, I was completely at ease. I really didn't care what we did, as long as we could hold hands and walk together or ride by his side in his truck and talk. I honestly just enjoyed being with him. I also loved the way he made me laugh and feel all warm inside. And of course, I was looking forward to my first make-out session with Hunter. Perhaps more, perhaps not more, at least for now. I was still taking matters in my own hands when I realized Hunter was being a bit of a flirt.

"Blah blah blah Ferris wheel down by Navy Pier blah blah blah Taste of Chicago at Grant Park. Or maybe I could give you some more pointers on your golf grip and swing. I would like to think we seem to fit pretty well together when I have my arms around you and hold you close. Wouldn't you say so, Leigh?"

I imagined his hard body up against mine and his strong, muscular arms snaked around me as he kissed my neck between whispering in my ear. "Ohhh, yess!" And that was that. I still don't know if he caught my actual response as I envisioned a complete pornographic version of his golf lesson.

"So it's a date! I'll pick you up Friday at noon!"

"Sounds awesome—see you then." I tried not to pant as I caught my breath.

We said our goodbyes and after I hung up the call I looked at Luna. "Yay! Now where the hell did he say we were going? I haven't the slightest idea what to dress for."

"Meow, meow."

"Easy for you to say."

"Meow."

"I know, that was pretty naughty of me. One way phone sex."

"Meow, meow."

"I'm not ashamed! A little dirty, yes, but not ashamed. Besides, you're a cat. You don't know what shame is. I've seen how you lick yourself."

"Meow."

Chapter Seven
Diddlers on the roof

Friday was soon approaching and I had to stop avoiding Kelly and Lindsey. To be honest, I did have some curriculum work I needed to finish up before it was due to be submitted for the upcoming academic year. I pride myself on being on top of things professionally, even if my personal life is unraveling like a cheap sweater. Despite the groaning protests of my friends, I used it as an excuse that they had to at least respect, somewhat. I had a good reason to avoid the super stalker issue. Without Gertie, I knew I could land myself in some trouble I really didn't need. I called out, I meditated, and I even asked Luna for help. Still, Gertie never showed.

I had been cautioned by the union about using magic on my own for now. Still, desperate times call for desperate measures and sometimes it's easier to beg for forgiveness than to ask for permission. Just ask any kid and they will confirm it. I couldn't blow off my best friends any longer. If there was hell to pay for unauthorized magic, I could deal with that later.

Gertie had gone back to her crazy cat farm and I had no idea how to reach her. It would have to be a good enough excuse to use magic, if I needed to. The witches at the union were equally unavailable to me, and my friends were in a state of desperation, apparently. I had made up my mind that I was going to use some witchy magic to solve Kelly and Lindsey's little stalker issue and put it all behind us, once and for all.

As promised, I finally headed out on Thursday to pay my friends a visit. Ever since my last conversation with

Hunter, I had already come to refer to Thursday as Hunter's Eve. I was so looking forward to our date that I actually caught myself using those very words in my head. My first stop was at Kelly's place, a small, one level duplex in a quiet neighborhood. Just before I left, I called Kelly and she mysteriously told me to park my car and wait for her in the alley that ran behind her house. I drove slowly down the tree lined street and past her place. There wasn't a single curtain opened and it looked as if nobody was home. I went part way around the block then cautiously up the alley until I neared the backside of her duplex. Kelly's back door opened slightly, and I could see her peeking out. Once she was sure that everything was clear, she jogged out to the alley and into my car.

"So, Kelly, what's this fugitive act all about?"

"My new neighbor. He's a complete perv. The guy won't leave me be. I would like nothing more than to have a restraining order slapped on him. But I doubt it would do any good considering our homes are attached. He likes to flash me every fucking chance he gets. It wouldn't be so bad, but he reminds me of the Pillsbury Dough Boy, complete with a two inch hard on. Ugh, the thought alone makes me want to vomit. Now let's get over to Lindsey's, then maybe you can see for yourself what we are dealing with here."

"Good idea. So far I haven't noticed a problem at all. Are you sure you guys aren't exaggerating just a little?"

"Just drive. You'll see soon enough."

We drove away with me thinking this entire situation was blown way out of proportion. After a short drive, we were in Lindsey's driveway. "Now take a good look." Kelly said as she observed some commotion on Lindsey's roof. There was Derek and Luke, both of them dripping with sweat and nearly ready to drop from heat exhaustion.

"Uh—what the hell? I thought this was a stalker problem, not a medical emergency in the making."

"You may not remember, but at some point you described the guys as hot roofers. If they aren't up there, they are busy obsessing over us."

"Hi, Kelly!" Shouted Luke. "I was hoping you would be coming over. Man, it sure is hot out. You know what to do, baby."

"Give me a minute, Luke. I'm on it." Kelly strolled on to Lindsey's front yard and picked up a spray nozzle that was connected to a garden hose. She shot a cold jet of water onto the roof, hitting Derek and Luke directly. She looked at me and said, "This has been the routine lately."

"Do they have any idea that they are acting so weird?"

"Oh, that's the thing! They do know that something is wrong, and I am pretty sure it scares the hell out of them, although they would never admit it to us. We've asked them why they are on the roof, after all, the job is done now. They can't explain it. Like an out of control compulsion to just climb up there and sweat their balls off."

"What about the stalker stuff?"

Lindsey had heard our arrival and stepped onto the front porch to watch the hose down of the boys. "They really are hot, though. I mean that in the sexy way. Just look at 'em. Jesus!" Lindsey watched wide eyed at the dripping wet hunks on her roof. To my surprise, she glanced back at her neighbors' houses across the street and then turned back to the boys. "Okay, boys, off with the jeans. Boxers only! You don't want heat stroke!" Derek and Luke kicked off their boots and jeans and were then on full display in soaking wet boxers. "Leigh, look across the street. See that blue house with someone looking out of a second floor window?"

I looked at the house Lindsey pointed out and I saw someone watching the rooftop strip show. Kelly was having fun with the hose. She had it set to the full jet setting and was doing her best to get the guys right in the boxers.

"Surprisingly, shrinkage doesn't seem so much of an issue for them." I observed.

"I know! I have to admit, this is the fun part!"

"What's your peeping neighbor doing? Is she going to call the cops or something?"

"Oh, heck no. That's Stephanie. Her husband is out of town a lot on business and she has three little wildcat kids at home. Sometimes she watches from the yard, but when she is peeking out of her bedroom window, I am pretty sure she is friggin' the hell out of herself." We all busted out in laughter. "You're welcome, Steph!" Lindsey called out to her and the curtains fell shut.

"Who's that?" I nodded to another lady about my mother's age. She came out and sat in a comfortable wicker chair on her porch.

"That's Jan. She is a sweetie. And she doesn't give a damn what anyone says, she is out to watch the show. Twice now her husband came out to join her and give her a backrub while she was getting off on the visual display. They are a trip." Lindsey waved to Jan, who returned her wave and gave her a thumbs up signal.

Kelly shut the water off and then told the guys to pack it up. "It's going to be sundown pretty soon. You should both be cooled down now. Why don't you come on down for the night?" The boys grabbed their things and made their way down the ladder. The neighborhood was filled with a variety of sounds that signaled disappointment from more spectators than just Stephanie and Jan.

Derek and Luke jogged to their truck and shot out a few apologies to us. Luke plead for sympathy. "I'm really sorry. I don't know what's wrong with us!" We watched as their truck sped away down the street.

"That's it? Doesn't seem all that bad to me! I'm sure your neighbors would agree." I commented.

"Oh, just wait. Let's go inside and forage for some food, and after a little while, you will see what else we've been dealing with." Lindsey beckoned us to follow her into the house.

"So, Leigh. Have you heard from Hunter lately?" Kelly had her entire head inside Lindsey's fridge and her voice was muffled. "I'm looking forward to snagging that stud. Lindsey, are you running some sort of clandestine penicillin operation in here? I don't think there is any kind of food that is supposed to be gray and fuzzy."

I was happy to reply to Kelly's inquiry. "Yep! Just today after you guys left. He called and asked me to go into the city with him tomorrow afternoon."

Kelly popped out of the fridge and gave me a genuine smile. "Really? That is awesome, Leigh. Really, it is. You know I was just kidding you about snagging Hunter."

"I wasn't." Lindsey plopped down in a chair.

"Well, no matter. I am looking forward to my date with him and I am hoping to bump things up just a notch, if you know what I mean."

"What you need to be bumping up is getting Luke and Derek back to normal. Maybe then we could all have some dating action for the summer." Lindsey was obviously getting frustrated. "Can't you just call Gertie and ask her to at least try that spell she thought about"

"I have no idea how to even get in touch with—" Just then we heard music coming from the front lawn.

"Okay. This is what we have been talking about." Kelly pointed to the window that faced the front yard.

The music was awful. It was a combination of two completely different types, and both types were being played very loud. I put my hands over my ears and shouted to my friends, "What the hell is that? It sounds like a pack of Tasmanian devils gang-raping a chimpanzee!"

Kelly was quick to describe what was happening outside. "Luke is reenacting something he saw in some old teen movie. You know, where the brokenhearted boy plays some stupid song on a giant boom-box to the girl-of-his-dream's house. Derek has an electric guitar and he's been playing some God awful song he wrote."

"My God. It's like karaoke night at the insane asylum."

"Oh, this is nothing. Last night Derek was trying out bagpipes. You can't serenade with bagpipes." Lindsey added. "And poor Luke's boom-box was set to an FM station that night. So instead of a sappy love ballad, it started to blare out that death metal stuff accompanied by Derek's bagpipes. Scared the bejesus out of me. I was actually shaking."

"Okay. Okay. I get it. This is a living nightmare. I can fix this, and I will fix this tonight, as soon as I get home. I'm not even waiting for permission from any other witches." Home is exactly where I went as fast as I could get there.

Chapter Eight
Back to the Magic Desk

When I opened my door, I was greeted by Luna. She seemed very excited to see me and once I was in the door, she bolted straight up onto my desk. Now, I know some people don't believe cats have special powers, extra senses, whatever you want to call them, however, I have always believed they do. Luna seemed to have been anticipating my arrival and that I had my mind set on getting some writing done. Writing that would hopefully return Derek and Luke back to the regular college boys we had first met.

I pulled up the file that I had written about my parents' recent garden party. I figured all I would need to do is add a few things to carry the story a little bit longer about the two werewolf hunters and their dates. No use in changing anything, what's done is done, and even Gertie affirmed that it was too late to reverse it. Luna encouraged me with a loud "meow" and ran her tail across my keyboard. I stroked her fur and smiled at how Luna sure loved anything related to witches.

After Luke and Derek left the party with their dates and enjoyed a fun evening out, the handsome young men received an urgent call. They had some more urgent and mysterious matters that needed to be attended to. Luke and Derek rushed off to hunt another pack of renegade wolves –

I was interrupted by the phone, the ringtone told me it was my sister, Sarah, calling.

"Hi, Sis. What's up?"

"I was wondering if you've talked to Mom and Dad lately."

"No. As a matter of fact, I usually hear from them once a week at a minimum, but I've been doing a little traveling lately. It's entirely possible I missed a call from them this past week. Why do you ask? Is everything okay?"

"Well, nothing bad. It seems like they have really renewed their romance lately. I've called twice this week and both times I swear I interrupted them in the middle of something. If you know what I mean."

"Oh, God, yes! I was over there this past week for a cookout. I walked in on our mother—I can't even say it."

"What?"

"Let's just say I walked in on them doing something in the kitchen of all places and it might take years for me to forget about. And it's enough to convince me they've renewed their passion."

"Wow! Well, thank God I haven't been there to have to witness anything like that. Anyway, it's given me an idea. Their big thirtieth anniversary is coming up. Maybe Mom read another book about rekindling their fire or some crap. Anyway, I think it is very sweet and we ought to do something for their big anniversary this year. Thirty years is a long damn time to be married."

"Yeah, thirty years is a long time. That's considered a life sentence I think. What do you have in mind? And don't say they should take a cruise."

"I don't know. Maybe renew their vows? I just wanted to plant that bug in your ear, see if we can come up with some ideas in the coming weeks. We are way overdue to come home, and it would be nice for the kids to spend some time with their grandparents."

"I'll keep it in mind. We can probably come up with something. How about you and your hubby? How is everything in the romance department since the ER visit?"

"Nothing. Leigh, it is really lousy. Ever since that fiasco, Bill has had—well, you know how guys can get. He is having some performance anxiety. Who can blame the poor man? And to make it worse, I started reading that erotic book that everyone seems to be reading lately. That BDSM erotica about the SEAL with amnesia, get this— the title is, *Bound to Forget*."

"Oh, *that* book. Yeah, I've heard about it, soft-core BDSM, graphic sex, a SEAL with amnesia, not really my thing." I was lying my ass off as I looked at the well-worn book on my night stand.

"Not my thing either, I guess. The only reason I read it is because the BDSM stuff is really just very mild foreplay action. Nothing too crazy. Still, it's been driving me up the wall, because I sure as hell am not getting any. I don't know why I'm telling my little sister this."

I knew she was lying her ass off, too. She never would have mentioned that book if it wasn't "her thing."

"Uh, yeah—but you are talking about *that* book, Sarah. So, go on."

"I was wondering if maybe you had any ideas. You know, to get him back on track."

"Hah. You're asking your little sister for sex advice? I can count the number of my sexual partners on just one of Luna's paws and still not use all of her little toes. And I'm not so sure that a couple of those technically qualify as sex since they lasted less than three minutes. My latest date nearly ended with me putting a guy in the ER!" I remembered what happened to Sarah and Bill with their own ER visit over a sex session gone awry. "Sorry, I didn't mean that to make fun of your recent—incident. Seriously, it didn't go well. And sex is something I've learned is best handled alone. Hell, it's been so long that I'm going to have to start referring to myself as a virgin again." I realized how pathetic I sounded, but it was all true.

"Sorry, Leigh. I just thought a young, single, and attractive woman like you would be all up to date on those goddamn Cosmo sex columns. Which totally suck by the way. I've tried reading them and I end up spending most of the time trying to figure out if it was written by one of the those twenty-five clowns that climb out of a tiny car at the circus. You know what I mean? How the hell do they do it?" Sarah started laughing. "I have to confess, I took two of little Adam's bendable toy people and tried to recreate one of those hot new positions step by step. It was like a goddamn human Rubik's Cube. Straight in the trash with that one. I want good sex, not some fucking circus act."

"Well, Sarah, how about this idea. Maybe there is something in that book you mentioned, *Bound to Forget*. You could pick a scene from it and reenact it with Bill. Or maybe you could read it with him. Just tease him a little, and that way you can let him know what you have in mind."

"You know, that's not a bad idea! There is a scene in the book where the woman ties her lover down on the bed. She teases the hell out of him, makes him beg for it, she wants to drive him to the point where he is just crazy with passion. And get this, she uses a small whip on him. I think it's called a riding crop. She drips hot candle wax on him! For some reason the thought of it is driving me mad. I just don't know how I could ever get him to agree to something like that."

"Well, like I said, start leaving him some hints. Read sections of the book to him. I don't know what all is in the story, I'm not really interested in anything too kinky. I think it's perfectly okay if it happens to a character in fiction, but quite another to act on any of it." I hoped like hell my sister didn't see through my lies. I didn't want her to think her baby sister was one of the biggest freaks on the planet.

"Okay, Leigh, but someday you'll be married and after you have a litter of kids, you will be proud of your household, your husband, and your children. Then you will learn that it has cost you something. That something will be your sex life. Unfortunately, you will find out that sex can become a bore, a chore, or just impossible to arrange. For example, we used to play a DVD of kid's TV shows to keep the little ones occupied long enough for us to squeeze in a quickie. It became the norm for us. Now whenever that show comes on TV and that schmuck starts singing, 'Who lives in a pineapple under the sea,' I start to get all wet and Bill gets a hard-on. It's like Pavlov's fucking dogs. Quite embarrassing, especially when you have company over and that show comes on. And if it should be playing when you are walking through the electronics section at Target? God forbid. Who wants to rely on that kind of stimulus to set the mood? Not exactly the type of romance a couple needs in their marriage. That's why women like me are interested in spicing things up. Oy! I don't know why I bothered you with it. Anyway, keep that anniversary idea in mind. It would be great if we could give Mom and Dad something really special this year."

After we hung up, I picked up my copy of the very book she referred to. I had read it, well, parts of it. Certain pages were even dog-eared for ready reference. I just didn't want to have a conversation about kinky fantasies with my sister. Seriously, it is one thing for me to talk about sex with my sister and quite another to reveal to her anything that might be considered a little off the beaten path. She's my sister and we have a history of ratting out each other's secrets for optimum embarrassment. In any case, I knew exactly what chapter and page she was talking about.

I knew just what I wanted to do for my sister. This was going to be one of my screw-the-rules moments and I easily justified what I was about to do. *Hell, I'm already breaking the rules by writing about Derek and Luke, I may as well hook up Sarah and Bill. After all, their last romantic debacle was all my fault. I owe them something.* I went back to crafting my magic.

I read over the basic ideas from the particular smutty chapter and announced to Luna, "I've got it."

"Meow, meow, meow."

"No problem. I'll even be sure to cover any possible problems that could arise. You know, safety issues. I don't want any complications."

Sarah led her blindfolded lover, Bill, to the waiting bed to satisfy her unfulfilled fantasy. Everything she did had the sole purpose of creating an erotic tease. She wanted to play on Bill's senses until he begged for more, and he wouldn't get that until he had been properly worked up into a state of complete animal like hunger for her.

For that night only, Sarah's fantasy blossomed before her and to her imagination Bill was a hot Navy SEAL. Toned and hardened in all the right places.

She double checked the handcuffs to make sure the keys worked properly and then she had Bill lie down on his back. Each handcuff carefully secured his arms to the spindles on the headboard. Once she knew he was comfortable and yet imprisoned, she placed the keys on the nightstand in plain sight, just in case there were any problems. Bill was already excited and drooling with anticipation for what he was about to receive at Sarah's hands.

She teased his naked body with a feather and then with a small leather whip, using only the lightest touch so as to not leave a single mark on him.

"Okay, so far, so good. I think, I am keeping this pretty safe. Wouldn't you say so, Luna?"

"Meow, meow." Luna pushed a small scented candle on my desk.

"Oh, yeah! Thanks for the reminder. Just one more thing and they should be worked up enough to handle it from there without any magic."

Bill was now completely aroused, but Sarah demanded that he beg for it, plead for it with more urgency to be set free in order to sate both of their primal needs. She brought a lit candle and dripped a little hot wax on his chest. He begged to have her. She dripped some more of the wax down over his stomach and inside his thighs. He was begging with all of his might for her to be merciful and set him free upon her in an animalistic frenzy.

"There! They are big kids. They can handle it from that point. Do you think animalistic is a word?"

"Meow, meow, meow."

"You worry too much, Luna. Nothing could go wrong with that."

Chapter Nine
An Unexpected Visitor

Friday had finally arrived. I was up and bouncing with excitement. I really needed to talk to Hunter. I simply needed to ask him what I should be dressed for. Inside? Outside? I had no idea, even though it had been discussed, in-depth you could say. I just wasn't paying much attention to the details that night as I was soaking in the bath. I worried that if I called him, he would think I was more of an airhead than I had already portrayed myself to be. I thought about it and remembered a bit of advice that I always tell other people. You may as well let people know exactly who they are dealing with sooner rather than later. If you come off as a scatterbrain or worse, so be it. People will get to know you one way or another.

"Hunter? Just me, Leigh."

"I was just thinking about you!"

"Yes! That's the kind of thing I love to hear! I hope it was all good thoughts."

"Of course! I was just going to call to see if you still wanted to go out today?"

No use in playing it coy. "Heck yeah! I've been looking forward to it. What would you like to do?"

"It is the Fourth of July, so how about we hit the Taste of Chicago down at Grant Park and then head over to Navy Pier. If we aren't too worn out, we can watch the fireworks later on. Have you ever been to the Taste of Chicago?"

"Wow, you know I had completely overlooked that it was the Fourth! No, I've heard of it. I know it has been going on this week, and it would be a lot of fun."

"Sounds great. See you at noon."

I now had exactly four hours to get ready, which gave me plenty of time to straighten out my apartment a little so I could invite him in for a bit before we go. That only takes fifteen minutes in my place. I had to pick out the perfect outfit, which I figured would kill a good hour at a minimum. Then there was getting the perfect hair, nails, and other tiny details that needed to be accomplished, two hours at most. I skipped the cleaning, he had already seen that I am not too overloaded with clutter. And that comes from being an organized elementary teacher.

I walked into my bedroom to browse through my closet when I heard what seemed like a small explosion from the coat closet by my front door. *What the hell was that?* Luna shot out of my bedroom and went towards the front door. I cautiously followed her. It was readily apparent to me what had happened once I noticed the pink and purple smoke seeping out under the closet door.

"Gertie? Is that you?" There was quite a bit of noise that sounded like the rattling of tangled clothes hangers combined with the thumping sounds of someone trying to fumble the door open.

"Hi, Leigh!" It was definitely Gertie's high pitched squeak. I opened the closet door and she stumbled out. She picked up Luna and nuzzled her. "Hi there, Luna." She set Luna down and immediately hugged me.

"Gertie! What happened? Are you all right?"

"I'm sorry, I really haven't gotten this traveling spell down very well, yet. I missed the front door somehow. Whoever thought to put another door so close to the front door certainly wasn't a witch. And I'm really sorry to barge in like this unannounced. Remind me that I have to get your phone number! Anyway, I'm here to help you out with your magic, to see if we can fine tune it a bit. Maybe we can help each other with that." Gertie looked at the closet and laughed. "I also want to tell you everything I know about witches, it may not be a lot, but I am sure I can answer some of your questions."

"That would be great! Umm—listen, I'm sorry, but I'm getting ready to head out for the day. I have a date."

"Oh! No, I'm sorry! I can come back another time, I suppose. The thing is that I only have this weekend free. I have to get back to my pussy—I mean, my cat plantation by Sunday."

"Well, I tell you what. Remember Kelly and Lindsey? I can check to see if they are free today. I know they would love to keep you company, and later on we can get together." I thought about the slim but very hopeful possibilities with Hunter, and then I added a built-in excuse. "That is if it doesn't get too late for me getting back from the city. In that case, I'll catch up with you in the morning."

"That would be fabulous! I was hoping to see those gals again." Gertie pulled out a small, lime-green Samsonite suitcase from the closet. She was dressed in her signature look, the bright floral patterned sleeveless summer dress and bright peach colored sandals. After another surprise hug, I pried Gertie's small frame off of me and made a call.

"All set! Kelly and Lindsey are thinking about going to some shindig at the park. It's out in the West suburbs, near Kelly's parents. They'll be by to pick you up, hopefully before I leave with Hunter."

"Lindsey had also told me that Derek and Luke had suddenly stopped stalking." I was pretty confident that my magic had worked. Still, I didn't want to jinx myself and say anything more about it. I had learned to wait for the other shoe to drop with this sort of thing.

"Can I get you some coffee or tea? Are you hungry?"

"Tea would be perfect! And I brought you a little surprise." Gertie knelt down and opened her suitcase. Like a surreal matador waving a floral patterned cape, she swung one of her summer dresses in front of her. "What do you think? I know it will be a perfect fit."

"For me?" I must have looked puzzled, but the dress was actually very cute. Bright floral patterns were definitely the in thing this summer, and I loved the cut. "Wow! Thank you. It's awesome!"

"I've been working as a seamstress since I was a little girl. Back then there was no such thing as a childhood. It was more of an apprenticeship. I knew your exact size after the first time I hugged you. I have dresses for Kelly and Lindsey also. They are each a little different, but very much the same."

"I'm going to try this on right now." I quickly stripped and pulled on the dress. Gertie came behind me, zipped up the back, and then adjusted the material a little. "You're right. A perfect fit. Amazing." It was perfect for my date with Hunter. "I am wearing this today!"

"Thanks. I'm so grateful to be in this day and age. Life is so much better, especially for women and children. And convenient! I could just go on and on about it, but I think you can imagine. Anyway, material and patterns like these are just one little example." Gertie stood back a little and looked me over. "I still have so many questions, so much to learn about things in these modern times. I hope you and the other girls don't mind me asking a lot of questions."

"Of course not, after all, what are friends for?" I stepped into the kitchen and brought a glass of iced tea out for Gertie.

"Oh, thank you. And please, I hope you don't mind, but could you do me a favor sometime and show me around? Would you mind? It's my old hometown, and I don't even recognize anything. What area is this again?"

"Technically, it's Franklin Park, my parents live in Skokie, not that far away, but with traffic on some days it might as well be the dark side of the moon. If you guys are out today, Kelly would be a good guide, she is from this area. Lindsey on the other hand is originally from a little farm area in Wisconsin, she is always getting lost. So never count on her for directions." I was interrupted by the incessant honking of a car horn. "That would be Kelly and Lindsey." I said, and ran to the desk, quickly jotting down a note for my friends. "And I'm sure they would love to help you out with anything, also. Please give Kelly this note for me? I'll see you later. Take care and have fun!" Gertie picked up her little suitcase and skipped out the front door to catch her ride. A thought crossed my mind that perhaps Kelly and Lindsey might not be the best influences for the naïve little witch. That was exactly what my note to my friends had cautioned them about. To take it easy on the poor girl. My guilt for pawning poor Gertie off on them had been absolved, and now I had more important issues on my mind.

Chapter Ten
Falling in Love

I happily prepared for my date. By the time I was finally ready, it was close to noon. Hunter showed up right on time and he looked great. He was wearing khaki shorts and a polo. While I donned Gertie's gift. It was seriously the perfect outfit for the day. Now there is no better compliment you can get than when it came the way Hunter delivered it. When I opened the door, his eyes widened, and the look on his face told me that he genuinely meant what he said. "Wow! You look great, Leigh!" And that made me blush. "It's just so great to see you again." That made me blush a little more.

I know that I don't have the cover-girl perfect body, and who really does? I feel comfortable being who I am, and when a guy like Hunter, or should I say especially Hunter compliments me, it only reinforces my self-confidence. It's the rare moments like those that I know I could care less about trying to meet someone else's unrealistic expectations. If someone put me on a magazine cover, they would be airbrushing the hell out of me. My legs would be too short for them, or my facial features too round, my tummy not quite flat enough, and so on. In any case, I'm sure you'll agree with me when I say that a girl never gets tired of flattery from the guy she is interested in. Never.

"Thank you, Hunter. And I'll be honest, I've been looking forward to this day all week." We both stood there smiling at each other like two squirrels staring at a mirror. I suppose if anyone saw us they would think we were quite nuts. "Oh, sorry, come on in. I'll just make sure Luna has fresh water and some food, then we can be on our way." Luna wasn't worried about her food, her water, or anything for that matter. Hunter had picked her up, and the little slut purred away while snuggled up against his chest. "Unbelievable, that cat! A month ago she would have been tearing your face off, now look at her."

Finally, we were out the door. I looked back and saw Luna staring out of the front window at us. I have to admit that she looked very sad, but also a little scary. It was almost as if she were jealous. Once we were on our way to Grant Park, I shook off the uncomfortable look I had gotten from my cat. It was a beautiful summer day and I felt great to be where I was, right next to Hunter. It was made even better when he asked me if I'd like to sit in the center of his truck's bench seat, right next to him. It was cozy and I could feel the heat of his body next to mine. I can't think of anything that turns me on more than the subtle and innocent—yet not so innocent—way that he can get close to me.

The radio had broken into the holiday traffic report. The continual updates on traffic are an absolute necessity for anyone that attempts to drive the congested toll ways of the Chicago area. Hunter turned up the radio and listened intently. "Did you hear that?"

"No, sorry, I wasn't really paying attention. What is it?" Of course I wasn't paying attention to the radio. I was too busy soaking up Hunter's sexiness.

"Something is happening over at the Lincoln Park Zoo. An incident of some kind. Not that it'll be a problem for us, I was going to get on the Eisenhower Expressway and turn up towards Grant Park. So, I think it's far enough from where we'll be. It really sounded bizarre. I wonder if it's one of those animal rights terrorist groups."

"What? What do you mean?"

"They said that the police had Lincoln Park Zoo and several blocks around it on lockdown. Apparently a couple of guys broke into an enclosure and tried to let out some animals or steal them—something like that. Sounds like it got a little out of hand. The guys are on the run and so are some of the animals. So now there are two crazy men being chased by animals and the police through Lincoln Park. Isn't that the weirdest thing?"

"Huh. That *is* bizarre." Something made me a little uneasy and at the time I couldn't put my finger on it, but I did my best to dismiss it. I suppose I wasn't about to let anything ruin my day. "Probably it's just some sort of fraternity boy prank gone wrong. Oh well. Hey, Taste of Chicago is happening after all. Maybe the zoo critters just want to sample the humans!" Hunter laughed at my little joke, and I laughed with him, a very uneasy little laugh.

"Well, I'll be sure to keep you safe."

We made our way down to the crowded area of Grant Park and the number of people packed together for the Taste was mindboggling, even for Chicago. Nearly every restaurant in the city had a tent or food trailer set up to offer samples of their respective culinary specialties. Commonly known to us Chicagoans as *The Taste*, it really is like a giant summer block party. The atmosphere always seems upbeat and if nothing else, Chicago knows how to put on a party. Hunter and I wandered about and tried a little of everything, always supplied in little paper cups. Hunter's plan was to see if we could go alphabetically and I agreed. Our appetites came to a halt when we hit the Cajun alligator. I had heard that alligator tasted like chicken, but all we could taste was a five alarm red hot pepper seasoning. All I can say about it is there is no *good* way to spit out red hot sauce in front of your date.

Our stomachs deserved a break and we wandered down to Buckingham fountain, one of Chicago's most well-known landmarks. We walked hand in hand and I could tell Hunter was really happy. We had been gradually dropping any of those early dating phase awkward feelings, but to be honest, I don't think there were that many to begin with, because of the way Hunter and I seemed to click. He's smart and funny as well. He is full of self-confidence without being a pretentious jackass. A very rare thing to find in men, in my opinion.

I had my purse well stocked with breath mints and I put them to good use for me as well as Hunter. I made sure to drink plenty of water to eliminate any lingering gator flavor, because I definitely was ready to sample another little taste of Chicago. Finally, we stood next to each other. I'm not so sure it was because we were so drawn to each other or more that we were *pushed* into each other by the teeming crowd. In any case, Hunter stood close to me. We were instantly lost in each other's eyes. I will never forget how he took one hand and swept my hair from my shoulder and ran it up behind my neck. His other hand reached around to the small of my back and then it happened. The kiss. The absolute kiss that shall forever be the benchmark that any other kiss will be measured by. For me at least.

My arms were wrapped up and around his strong shoulders and our lips met. He kissed me softly at first and I was expecting him to pull away, but he didn't. His kiss grew more passionate, and it was as if he could feel how I was responding, both physically and emotionally.

Before I knew it, our tongues danced together and we were completely lost to anything else that was happening. It was as if the crowd had simply vanished.

As it turns out, they did just that. When we finally stopped for a second, Hunter smiled at me and I was blushing. I had been hoping to someday be kissed like that, right there in front of Buckingham Fountain, and he nailed it. I'm not sure if it was Hunter or me who first noticed the screams fading in the distance as the hordes of Chicagoans scattered like a herd of frightened sheep. Sirens were wailing and the scene was nearly too much for me to handle.

"Hunter? What—what the hell is happening?" I was shocked by the sudden emotional switch from passion to panic.

"I don't know. I guess I wasn't paying atten—" Hunter stopped in midsentence and pointed to the fountain. "There! That!"

I expected to see a meteor screaming down towards us or an army of terrorists hell bent on destroying the city. In fact, it was neither. It was something so surreal that I couldn't comprehend what it was at first. Apparently the entire collection of primates from the Lincoln Park Zoo had escaped and they were on a rampage. When you see a lowland gorilla in a zoo, calmly munching on a carrot, you forget the creature weighs nearly five hundred pounds, and he could tear a human in half without breaking a sweat. Seeing a whole group of them trashing everything they could get their big meaty hands on was a frightening lesson in how scary a pissed off ape can be. A large silverback gorilla climbed to the top of Buckingham Fountain and beat his chest. Police, zookeepers, and city animal control officers were fanning out in the now emptied park. They used the abandoned mobile food venues for cover.

"Why don't they just tranquilize them?"

Hunter tried his best to calm me down and then pointed to a young man in tattered clothing, he was being dragged by another gorilla through the flower garden. Obviously alive, but badly shaken at the very least. "There, they want to save that guy." Hunter motioned for me to get down low to the ground. "We've got to get away, but I think if we try to run, those gorillas will be after us in a heartbeat. See that Thai food wagon?"

"Yeah, the one that's called *Thai Me Up*, I see it. You think we can make it?"

"We will make it, Leigh. Now crawl slowly and keep low. It's not far."

We crawled across the grass and made it to the trailer without being noticed. Once inside, Hunter shut the door and tried to secure it as best he could. The radio was left on and we listened to the breaking news story being broadcast.

"Officials are warning anyone in the Loop to seek shelter immediately while they deal with a situation that is as dangerous as it is bizarre. Police are describing this as an apparent eco-terrorism incident. It started earlier in the day at the Lincoln Park Zoo when Zoo security officials confronted two men who had broken into the red wolf exhibit and were attempting to abduct the wolves. They fled on foot through the zoo and were able to escape the property by hijacking a truck. Following a high speed chase involving several Chicago Police squads, the truck overturned on South Lakeshore Drive near Grant Park. The hijacked truck was carrying containers that housed several large African Lowland Gorillas. The animals escaped into Grant Park where the Taste of Chicago celebration is being held. Officials have said the gorillas are extremely unpredictable since they were recently recovered from a zoo in a war-torn area, and they are psychologically unstable. Now I don't think in my twenty years of broadcasting that I have ever had to describe a gorilla as psychologically unstable. Hold on, I'm just getting this in now. It appears the gorillas have indeed captured one of the suspects and have him near Buckingham Fountain. Police are saying his condition is unknown as is the whereabouts of the second suspect. Please, for God's sake people, stay clear of this situation. We will keep you updated as events unfold."

"Hunter? Hunter! Oh, thank God! Please, we have to save Derek!" A voice cried out from behind a pile of boxes in the back of the trailer.

"Luke? Luke? What the fuck? Derek? Were you the guys everyone is chasing? Including the pack of insane gorillas?"

"Yes, yes. I have no idea what happened. It's—it's like we were possessed or something. Like the devil himself made us go into the wolf enclosure and then we just panicked. I—I'm so sorry about all of it and I'm really worried about Derek."

"Holy shit! When you college boys decide to go crazy, you don't mess around." Hunter said and shook his head in dismay.

"I'm so sorry." I knew it, this was all my fault. I remembered what I wrote. Luke and Derek received an urgent call to go after some wolves. Where else can you find wolves in Chicago except in a zoo? And shit just went downhill from there.

"Leigh, you have nothing to be sorry for. Now this bonehead? He has something to be sorry for. I can't even begin to imagine how deep the shit is that he is in right now. Just stay in here, Leigh. I'm going to look outside and see what's happening." Hunter opened the door and peeked outside. "Good, the gorillas have left Derek alone. He's laying up against the fence by the fountain. It looks like the gorillas are heading back to Lakeshore Drive." Hunter paused his play by play description. "Good, the zoo guys are shooting them with tranquilizer guns now. Quick, come on Luke, let's go grab Derek." Luke pushed away the little wall of cardboard boxes that he built. As if the flimsy makeshift barricade would actually stop a platoon of deranged gorillas.

I watched Hunter and Luke run out to retrieve what I assumed would be Derek's corpse. To my surprise, Derek jumped up and ran full speed to the food wagon I was still hiding in. "Oh, Hi, Leigh! Sorry. I was playing opossum. Thank God, they're gone. That was a nightmare." Derek looked at his ripped clothing with an amazed look. His jeans were mere shreds of cloth. All that remained of his shirt was the collar and a flap of material hanging over his chest, as if he were wearing a bib.

When Hunter and Luke came back, Hunter berated the young roofers with a ferocity that was quite pleasant to observe. I may have bewitched them into going after the wolves, but stealing a truck full of crazed gorillas, well, that was all on them. Hunter chased them off with some advice. "I'm not a cop, yet. SO you two better run and run fast. If you get caught, confess. If you get away, you better tap those fat trust funds and send a huge ass donation to the zoo to cover the costs of the truck and more. If not, I promise I'll come after you." Hunter looked around the trailer and handed Derek one of the long gone cook's aprons to him. Derek put it on so that at least the front of his boxers were covered up.

Luke and Derek bolted away and disappeared in the distant clutter of more food trailers. I couldn't help but laugh at the scene. Shoeless Derek wearing a white apron with large red letters that said *Thai Me Up*, chasing after Luke through Grant Park.

Chapter Eleven
Serious Leigh

"Leigh, I have to say this. It is always an adventure when we get together. Have you noticed?"

"I'd say. Still, I wouldn't trade today for anything, Hunter."

"And neither would I. Not for anything."

Yes, it is absolutely true. The man melts my heart, like wax dripping from a burning candle. I was feeling something. Something bigger than I had ever felt for anyone. The only question I had for myself was one I really hated to contemplate. *How long before I screw things up too much with Hunter that he takes off like a bat out of hell?* I was determined for the rest of our Independence Day date to keep going. I was worried that Hunter was ready to just throw in the towel. Crazed apes in Grant Park? Seriously. Things could only get better from there.

The rest of our date was pleasantly uneventful. I made sure to avoid any situation that could prove disastrous. The giant Ferris wheel at Navy Pier? Out of the question. The last thing I wanted was to have that sucker become unhinged and have Hunter and me rolling away to our watery graves at the bottom of Lake Michigan. Even Hunter sensed a need to avoid danger. When he noticed the miniature golf course on the pier, he turned away from the ticket booth as if they were operating a do-it-yourself castration venue. We settled for the highly recommended Cirque Shanghai Warriors performance. I am happy to report it was an amazing act that we happily walked out of, fully intact. Of course, we missed a good portion of the performance with an epic make-out session that left me absolutely starving for much more of Hunter.

I was beginning to have some thoughts, naughty thoughts about what could come later on. I feigned sore feet and a slight headache, which played out perfectly. Forget the fireworks over the lake. The only fireworks I was interested in were the ones I hoped would be going off when Hunter would be making love to me. Yes, I had already mentally crossed that line and resigned myself to the fact that the Fourth of July was going to become Thanksgiving. I hoped Hunter would be giving and I would be thanking. If he did anything, even half as well as he could kiss, well, it was going to be a very special night. Hunter happily offered to take me home. I suggested a relaxing evening of television at my place. This was a more pleasant option than dealing with the late night traffic out of downtown.

Within an hour, we were pulling up in front of my apartment. Hunter and Luna made themselves comfortable in my living room, and after getting him something to drink, I excused myself for a bit. I stood in my bedroom and took a deep breath. *Okay, now what should I do?* I had so little experience in this matter. You could say that I didn't have any sexual partners. I had three one-time disappointments. No repeat performances from any of them. Scratch that, two. The first one came on my thigh and it was over, so I don't think that qualified. Number two was okay, but only for two or three minutes and it was over. Number three lasted *almost* long enough to be adequate, unfortunately, size was *definitely* an issue. I had expected it to grow a little bigger than my thumb and it never did. I sometimes wonder if the poor guy ever found a partner that would be okay with that *small* problem. Imagine having to adjust yourself just to feel that it was even in there. Eight minutes of disappointment on that try.

I was still trying to figure out what to do. Mental checklist. Protection? Yes, I was on the pill, speaking of which seemed so pointless. For the undersexed women like me taking a pill every day for safe sex was like buying a lottery ticket every day and never getting a dime back in return. Wash up a bit, no problem. What about clothes? I wondered if I should put on something sexy. No, I didn't want to come out to the living room looking like a professional. I could make some adjustments.

I called out to Hunter. "I'm just going to get into something more comfortable than this dress. Be right out!" Comfortable, that sounded better, comfortable with easy access. I dug out a skimpy bra and put it on. I looked in the mirror and fretted over the fact it always seemed to me that one breast was slightly lower than the other. Do guys care? Well, can't change that. Skimpy undies, sheer ones, yes that was perfect. Some loose shorts and a t-shirt. Now what? I wanted to text Kelly for advice, but that was like asking a florist for advice about cars. Lindsey? No. My failed sexual episodes could only be eclipsed by hers. My sister? I already knew how *that* would go. Something freakish and desperate. I resigned myself that if anything was going to happen, I'd be better off if I just give up a little control and let Hunter take the lead. I took one very deep breath and then another. With a fluttering heart, I went back to the living room.

Any fear that things would be awkward completely vanished when I saw Hunter. I sat next to him and he pulled me closer. He kissed me and his hands lightly explored my shoulders, neck, and the side of my face. Not to be outdone, I took a hand and felt his strong arms and then his chest. The moment was timeless and beautiful. He moved his mouth to my neck, and for me, it was the end of any subtle behavior. Full of confidence and sexual power, I stood up. I stepped close to him and straddled his waist, resting my knees on the couch. I leaned forward and kissed him while I unbuttoned his shirt, working my way down until it was free. I straightened up and he quickly took his shirt off and cast it aside. I could feel how incredibly hard he had become beneath me. It was impossible to stop myself from rocking on him just a little.

"Your turn." I took the cue and pulled my t-shirt up over my head. Then I let my hands freely explore his muscular upper body. I enjoyed admiring him like that, seeing and feeling the toned muscles of his chest, massive shoulders, and arms. He was thick and powerful, yet well defined. Not that I was tired of the view, but I couldn't hold myself back. I moved down to get lost in more of Hunter's kisses. I hardly noticed that his roaming hands had made their way to my back when he effortlessly unhooked my bra. We were taking our time, but there was one little bit of discomfort. His rock hard erection was pressing against the closed fly of his jeans and it felt a little rough through my skimpy shorts. I wanted to draw out our fun foreplay as long as possible, so while I kissed his neck, I undid the button of his jeans, just to give him a hint of what I had in mind. I slipped down to my knees and there between his legs I had his zipper right in front of me.

After I ran my hands slowly down his chest and rock hard stomach, I worked his zipper down. His cock was now straining against the cotton briefs and I ran my hand over it. This was the kind of thing I fantasized about, and obviously size was *not* going to be a problem. I adjusted it so that the head of his cock, and more, was now freely up against his stomach, all the way to his belly button. His hands were running through my hair, and with each passing minute he seemed to lightly urge my head downward. I knew what he wanted. I wanted to also, but why rush things? I used my tongue to trace the area around his stomach and came within a mere fraction of an inch of his throbbing wonder. I let my hair fall on it, I breathed on it, but I didn't touch it with my tongue. Then I stood up. In a low and husky voice, that didn't seem to sound like my own, I told him what I wanted him to do. "Take off those jeans, but leave your shorts on."

Hunter quickly got rid of his jeans. I took off my shorts, leaving just my sheer little panties on. I straddled him once again and resumed my earlier pleasure of rocking against him. With his mouth to my ear he whispered, "I like this game, my turn." He sat forward and lifted me right up. My legs hung on either side of him. He turned me around and placed me on the couch. Now he was the one kneeling down between my legs, and *I* was the one running my hands through *his* hair. The tables had turned, and I was the one to silently urge him to get down to what I hoped was my Fourth of July fireworks show.

His hands were on my breasts and his tongue gently flicked inside my thighs. He brought a hand down and pulled aside the skimpy cloth that covered my now soaking wet folds. His tongue drew ever closer to where I wanted it to be. I gasped out loud as his tongue parted the soft folds and found the nub it sought. With his tongue expertly caressing and dancing around, it became too much for me to bear. I pulled his head forcefully into me.

So, this is what it is supposed to feel like. I was lost in the perfect feeling until I wanted more. I let go of Hunter's head and as if he could read my mind, he removed the last remnant of my clothing. Before he could go back down on me, I sat up and went right for his hardness. I wanted to free it, I wanted to feel it. I worked his briefs down and then took him in my hand. Admiring his thickness and length, I stroked it and put my mouth on him. It felt so hot and erotic to be doing what I was finally able to do. I didn't want to waste the opportunity of this night by rushing anything. I was enjoying the fact that it made him feel like I had felt just minutes before. I was exploring every part of him. It felt like the best dream ever.

A loud crash came from the little hallway that led to my bedroom. I'm pretty certain we both assumed it was just Luna getting into some sort of mischief. Neither of us cared about it. Then more crashing that sounded like my shower curtain rod had been torn down. "Do you want me to check that out?" Hunter offered.

"Mmmm nnnnn" was all I could answer. Then out of the corner of my eye, I saw it. Little wisps of pink and purple drifting close to the floor from the hallway. *Gertie! Damn it!* I immediately stopped what I was doing. "Uh, I probably should check on Luna. Stay right here—and hold that thought for a minute." I tiptoed briskly into my hallway. I passed the bathroom and as I flicked on the light, I saw Gertie lying in the bathtub. She had one leg hanging over the side and the shower curtain covering everything else but her face. I had to whisper. "Gertie. Gertie." She seemed as if she was knocked out, or nearly so.

"Hi ya, Leigh!" Gertie smiled, shut her eyes and began to snore.

I could tell what was going on. "Drunk? You're drunk? What the hell? Ugh." Gertie was still smiling, but totally unresponsive.

Now, what to do. I could call my friends and tell them to pick up Gertie's drunk ass. She was my guest, after all, so that probably wasn't the right thing to do. I could force Gertie to wake up and have her poof herself back to wherever she came from, but in her condition, there was no telling where she would end up. Of course the right thing to do was to make up an excuse and have Hunter go home. I could make it up to him. At least I could hope to.

So I did what anyone in my completely still-turned-on situation would do. I shut the bathroom door and left Gertie passed out cold in my bathtub, and I went back over to Hunter. "Take me to my bed, please—I want you so bad." After all, I had the hottest piece of ass to ever look my way, naked in my living room, and one that I was falling head over heels for. A troupe of fiddle playing leprechauns could have marched through my living room and I *still* would have cared less. There was no way I was passing this up. Hunter carried me to my bed and never once glanced in the darkened bathroom. "Shut the door please. I don't want Luna in here right now." Hunter obliged and we returned to our lovemaking. I pushed Hunter back on the bed and went back to do exactly what I had been doing before I was interrupted. Only this time my legs were next to his face. As I hoped, he swung one of my legs over his head and he put his tongue back to work while my mouth and hands eagerly worked on his manhood.

I could hear Gertie begin to stir in the bathroom. I half expected her to come stumbling into the bedroom, but she had become oddly silent. *Passed out cold,* I thought to myself. I started to feel guilty when I considered that Gertie could have hurt herself when she fell, but that kind of guilt was difficult to muster up when one is in the middle of repeated orgasms. I again forgot all about Gertie after I thought, *maybe it's time to hurry things along.*

I rearranged myself on the bed next to Hunter and in a magical moment he took me in his arms. He was kissing my neck and holding me close when he began to penetrate me. It was wonderful, beautiful, and the most intimate moment of my life. Not just the fact that he was inside of me, but the way he held me and kissed me while he did it. Yes, there was nothing I could compare it to. Ever. I had no idea how long we went on. All I know is that when Hunter slowed down, I felt completely spent. My body had been shuddering over and over, and I felt things I had never felt.

"I know one thing, I've never made love before. This was amazing." Hunter whispered.

"I know exactly what you mean, I was about to say the same thing." I meant it. I know we both had experiences. Obviously, he had more experience than I did, but I believed him when he told me that because I could feel it, too. I stared into his eyes and thought about something very seriously. I had never been in love, and consequently, I had never had my heart broken either. Could that ever happen with Hunter? Would he be my first love *and* my first heartbreak? *No! Not if I can help it. I'll use magic on his ass, if it ever came to that. Well, maybe not. I don't know. I need to just savor this right now feeling. Still, I'd use magic on his ass anyway.*

"Leigh?"

"Yeah?"

"I just want to tell you something. I'm kind of falling for you. If you haven't noticed. Hard."

"Me too. It's a little scary, isn't it?"

"Not if we feel the same way."

And that made me feel fucking awesome. There was no other way to describe it.

Chapter Twelve
In Through the Out Door

I threw on my bathrobe and excused myself. I went to work quietly waking up Gertie. "Gertie! Gertie! Come on, get up."

She was seriously slurring her words. "Ohhhh yes, get up. I can do that." Gertie stood up, but her posture was as if she was walking on ice with an eighty pound backpack on. "Ooh. Gotta find my legs."

"Shhh, be really quiet and come with me." I held her up and walked her to the front door, which I very quietly opened. I walked her outside and she immediately sat down on the step.

"I—I—what?"

"Shhh just stay there." I rang my own door bell and jumped back inside. I then acted like I was surprised to get a late visitor.

"Gertie? What are you doing here?" I spoke very loudly so that Hunter would hear me now. "Oh and you're drunk? I can't believe this! Oy! Your friends just dropped you off like this?"

"Huh? No. Hey! Wasn't I juss inside? Why didja put me on the porshhhh?"

"Ach, you poor girl. Here sit down. You can stay here tonight."

Hunter walked into the living room with only a towel around his waist. "Is everything okay?"

"Yep. One of my friends was apparently celebrating the Fourth of July a little too hard and ended up on my porch. Hunter, meet Gertie O'Leary and Gertie, meet

Hunter Kovacs." I picked up Hunter's clothes and hoped that Gertie hadn't noticed when I handed them to Hunter.

"Why er ya naked? Hunterrr? Rrrr..rrr—I like the sounda yer name. Hunt err. You should come an see my Pussy Farm."

"Huh?"

"Never mind her, she's pretty drunk."

"No sheerishly, you oughta see it. I got all sorts a pussy. More kindsa pussy than you kin magine. Now, Leigh she's got her a nice pussy, I juss love that sweet lill pussy. Have you seen her sweet lill pussy?"

"Gertie means cats. She runs a shelter for cats. And she's talking about Luna." I laughed awkwardly.

"Oh! Sure, that makes sense now. Nice to meet you Gertie. Excuse me." Hunter went back down the hall to get his clothes on.

"Wow! Heeza nice one! Can you fine me one a them, like that?"

I waited for Hunter to make it back to the bedroom before I said anything more, once again talking in a hushed voice. "Gertie! What the hell happened to you tonight? Where are Kelly and Lindsey?"

"I dunno, but I sure hope they are makin more of that deshishus jello."

"Jello shots! Damn those girls."

"You know Kelly's mum? She makes the best punsh."

"Punsh? Oh, punch. That's her sangria. Her Dad didn't make you drink that stuff he calls *mojo*, did he?"

"Uh huh. I'm not feelin too good, Leigh."

Mojo was a concoction that Kelly's Dad, Benny, made by pouring any hard liquor he could get his hands on into a large cooler and added hunks of fruit and juice. I grabbed my phone and made a call to Lindsey. "What did you two do? Gertie crash landed in my bathtub tonight, and she's completely schickered!"

On the other end of the phone was an equally inebriated Lindsey and Kelly, and from the drunken laughter, I could tell they had me on speakerphone. They were still at Kelly's parents' house.

"Just promise me that you two will stay there tonight? Gertie will be fine here." I said.

Just then Hunter made his way back to the living room. Gertie propped her head on my shoulder and shouted into the phone. "Hey, guess what? Leigh has a man here, they are both naked! And guess what they were doing?"

Kelly and Lindsey then started cheering and it was obvious that everyone else in their proximity was listening to them. "Woo hoo! Leigh finally got laid! How was the Hunkster?" I hung up.

"Hunter, would you please help me get Gertie into the bathroom before she throws up on the carpet?"

"You have to share that spell you casted, Leigh. I really need a Hunter. You have no idea how bad I need one. Lemme tell you—*hiccup*—it's been over a shenshur—over a shenna—over a hunner years since I had some a that. Well, I've actually never had any of that." She slapped an open palm against Hunter's chest and then smacked his ass. "Well, maybe I'll get some a Kelly's big brother, Randy. I'll settle for some Randy Johnson."

"I bet you would, Gertie. I bet you would." After I said that, I just shook my head. There was more that Gertie would need to learn about Randy.

"Wow, she *is* drunk! She isn't making any sense." Hunter commented.

"Drunk you say? Jaysis, I'm ossified!"

"Gertie. What the hell do you mean, ossified—"

"Izz ish, izz irsh, izz what Irish says, means I'm too drunk to danz." Gertie started snoring.

"I'm sorry. I hope this hasn't ruined our night. It was so—"

"Incredibly awesome? That's how I would describe it. Like I said before, it's always an adventure with you. How about I let you take care of your friend. I'll call you in the morning. You can count on it."

"No, call me when you get home, so I know you made it back safely."

We kissed and at the same time we fumbled over our words. I finally said, "Thank you for such a wonderful day and evening. Could have done without the crazed gorillas, but it worked out okay."

With that, Hunter left for the night and I was left to take care of Gertie. Luna had reappeared, which I thought was rather odd that she had made herself scarce with two of her favorite people around. Luna followed us into the bathroom. I had Gertie splash some cold water on her face. I don't know of any cure for how she was feeling. The feeling that comes when you are too drunk to notice or care how sick to the stomach you truly are. "Poor Girl. I'm sorry that my friends got you in this condition."

I took Gertie's Barbie Doll sized broom out of her purse. After I stashed it in the medicine cabinet, I walked her over to the couch. I gave her a pillow and covered her with a blanket. She would be feeling this one in the morning, and that was a certainty. As for me, I curled up in my bed just in time to answer Hunter's call. At least we were able to say goodnight properly for at least an hour. And a little phone sex was definitely part of that conversation.

Chapter Thirteen
The Morning After

Saturday morning came in like a soft breeze, at least for me. As for Gertie, it had to have been like a freight train that had just derailed. Or so, I thought that's how she would have felt. Surprisingly, Gertie bounced back pretty quickly. I came in to the kitchen quietly and there she was brewing tea, making toast with peanut butter, and singing along to some upbeat top forty music that played on the radio. Quite loudly.

"Hi, Leigh! Sorry about last night. Your friends sure know how to make a girl feel welcome! And Kelly's parents sure know how to throw a party."

"Oh, that's for sure. I've been to a few of those." I had to be a bit of a downer. "Listen, Gertie. I have to tell you something. If you are going to drink, don't fly. Or whatever you call it. What if you wouldn't have landed in my tub? You could have ended up on the middle of the Tri-State Tollway! God forbid! There'd be nothing left of you! And besides, I don't think alcohol and any kind of magic is a safe mix. Do you?"

"No. No. You're right. I didn't even know I was getting drunk from the Jello. After a while, I had lost any common sense. Things got a little out of hand, I'm afraid. I just can't handle my liquor I suppose. Not as bad as Kelly's dad, though. To use her Mom's words, he was both 'Purim wasted' and "Columbus Day Hammered,' whatever that means."

"It means Benny was pretty damn drunk."

"Well, anyway, I had lost all self-control." Gertie said reluctantly.

"Oh no! No! Please don't tell me you used a magic spell over at the party?"

"Um—okay, I won't tell you. But it was my first time ever being drunk. I had no idea."

"Ugh, Gertie, now what? How bad is it?"

"Actually, I'm not sure yet. I don't even know if it worked. You see, we all went down to the horse track they have over there in—something Heights to watch some really incredible fireworks."

"Yeah, Arlington Park. It's a pretty major horse racing track right there in Arlington Heights. What the hell happened?"

"All I can say for sure is that Lindsey and Kelly dared me to do some things for those wonderful horses. Have I told you how much I just love animals? How boring it must be for them to just run around a circle, though. Anyway, I told the girls about my other business venture back home. It's kind of in the startup phase right now. I call it, *Gertie's Paranormal Pet Shop*. You see, I sometimes take in other stray animals, besides cats, at the Pussy Plantation, I mean Stray Cat Plantation, that's the new name by the way—"

"Wait. Paranormal Pet Shop? What do you mean?"

"The other stray animals. For example, I get a donkey. Who wants an old worn out donkey? Nobody! You can't give it away. But a unicorn, that's different. Who wouldn't want a unicorn? Or a Pegasus? Or say I take in a poor abused chimpanzee who was mysteriously rescued from a medical testing lab." Gertie looked down at her shoes and smiled. I knew damn well she had stolen some chimpanzee from a testing lab. "Well, who is going to take in a stolen chimp? Nobody. But a Sasquatch? They'll be knocking down the doors for one of those, I reckon. So far, I've been perfecting my spells, I haven't opened to the public just yet, but—"

"Oh, shit. What did you do to those racehorses?"

"Like I said, I was talking to the girls about it, and being drunk and all, we thought it would be fun to see a race with some special horses. Now, I don't know if it worked, but we'll probably know come the races today."

"Ugh! You mean to say there is going to be a damn unicorn running the track at Arlington Park today? Oy! What else? Pegasus flying overhead? A dragon scorching the people in their seats?"

"Of course not! Dragons are *way* too unpredictable. Peanut butter on toast?" Gertie held out a slice of toasted bread she had covered in a perfectly smooth layer of peanut butter. I reached out and then she stopped. "Wait, one more thing." She took the butter knife and traced a cute cat face on the toast and then handed it to me.

How could I resist her? I started to laugh at the situation. "Thanks." I slumped into a chair at my little dining table and Gertie brought me a cup of tea. "Unbelievable. Just unbelievable how this summer is going. Everything. From meeting Hunter and all that is happening with us, then this magic." I shook my head. "I'm mostly worried about screwing things up for me and Hunter, like it has for Luke and Derek with Kelly and Lindsey."

"Let me ask you this, Leigh. Did things always go perfectly well with guys before you knew you had the power of witchcraft? Was it always disaster free?"

"No, I suppose you're right. Guys, dating, that whole scene has been pretty much a series of train wrecks for all of us."

"Exactly my point. At least now the train wrecks are hopefully a little more entertaining. I think the only advice I have is to keep from upsetting those old witches in the union."

"Do you mind me asking what happened that you were frozen for the second time? If you don't want to talk about it, just say so. I won't bring it up again."

"No, it's okay. You deserve to know. I had just gotten thawed out from my misadventure with turning Chicago into a smoldering heap. I had befriended these wonderful harbor seals that live in the Arctic. Something terrible was happening to them. Polar bears. Those bears were just monsters. I won't even tell you how they behaved to the seals. I decided to use my magic and separate them from the seals. I waited until they were on a very large iceberg and I sent that thing away as fast as I could. I had no idea polar bears were such good swimmers, they simply jumped in the water and swam to another hunk of ice. I saw the big iceberg that I sent away float over the horizon. I never gave it another thought. Who knew that I had sent it on a collision course with the Titanic? Complete accident. Of course, I got the blame for that one. Even though those sailors should have paid better attention."

"Wow! The Chicago Fire and then the Titanic Disaster? Talk about a run of bad luck."

"Yes. Indeed. But I think of it as the best thing that ever happened to me. I mean being frozen for so long and not the fact that I had a hand in so many tragic deaths and all. Now I'm living in modern times and I would never want to go back to what life was like in 1873 or 1912. It was really awful compared to now, especially for women."

Our conversation was interrupted by the ringing of the phone. I eagerly grabbed the call, hoping it was Hunter.

Chapter Fourteen
Another Union Scroll

I didn't even look at my caller ID when I answered, I practically spit sunshine all over my phone. "Hello?"

Oh, it was Lindsey. I knew right then that I should change my ringtone to identify Hunter's calls. Well, at least I had every reason to expect calls from him. Lindsey picked up on the change of my tone.

"What's wrong?"

"Oh, nothing. I was hoping you were Hunter."

"Oh, yes, we'll all have to get the details on your date! It's so exciting."

"It was and it is! We can talk about that later, though. So what are you up to today?"

"It's a beautiful Saturday and holiday weekend. I'm cooking out at my place! Don't worry, I'm not planning on a repeat of the wild party like Kelly's folks threw last night. So be here around one-ish with Gertie. Oh, and if Hunter is free, it would be awesome if he could make it."

"Fine, but if he does, promise me that you guys won't ask him anything embarrassing?"

"Teacher's honor. One more thing. You must have done something to break the spell on Derek and Luke, we haven't heard or seen a thing from them."

"Oh, yeah! I did. Apparently it worked. There was some slight backlash from that, though. Did you see the news yesterday?"

"Something about animal rights terrorists at Lincoln Park Zoo? They let the gorillas loose in Grant Park or something crazy."

"That was the backlash I was talking about. They weren't terrorists, Lindsey. It was Derek and Luke. They were charmed into capturing a few wolves. That was just some incidental thing I had written into the story to get them off your backs. Next thing I know, they are breaking into the zoo, stealing a truck full of psycho gorillas, and going on a high speed chase down Lakeshore Drive. They crashed and had to run from the police *and* the gorillas. Hunter and I were right there in Grant Park when it all went down. Your boys got away. I don't know if the authorities identified them, though."

"Holy shit! That was them? That was all your witchcraft?"

"Please, don't say it like that. You know I didn't mean for any of that to happen."

"Sorry. I know, Leigh. I miss them already. So does Kelly. Do you think you could please, please get them back for us. Just not with all the crazy obsession stuff? Can Gertie help you?"

"I'll see what I can do, Lindsey. I just hope those poor boys don't end up committed to a psych ward by the end of this summer."

After the call, I turned to Gertie and told her of the plan for the day. "Seems like we have a cookout to attend at Lindsey's. And I hate to say this, I also need your help with a little magic."

"Magic! Now we're talking! What do you have in mind?"

"Remember the super stalkers that Kelly and Lindsey were dealing with?"

"The hot roofers?"

"Yep! That's the guys. They are also the werewolf hunters in *Four-Bitten Fangtasy*. Because of their characters in the story, they became completely devoted and obsessed boyfriends. The other day I decided to write some more and have Luke and Derek get an urgent message to go after some wolves. You know, get them onto something other than the girls. Well, what happened to them is a real mess. In any case, Lindsey and Kelly actually liked having the guys around. They want them back, just not in restraining order style. They want them to be normal, if that is even a possibility. I'm thinking of having them return to the girls, now that they've completed their mission. I just want you to look over what I write to see if you can spot any possibilities that it could be taken the wrong way."

"Sounds simple to me, Leigh. Let's do it." Gertie said. I led her over to my desk to watch as I continued the story of Derek and Luke.

Derek and Luke had successfully completed their wolf hunting expedition and now had their girls, Kelly and Lindsey, back on their minds. Things had changed. Perhaps it was the danger they encountered on their adventure, or maybe it was just the time they spent away. Whatever the reason, Derek and Luke both agreed they had been too obsessed with their girls in the past. They wanted to still date them at a completely normal and natural pace. They vowed to be polite, well behaved, and courteous to Lindsey and Kelly while still being very romantically interested in them.

"There. Done. Now read this over very carefully. Look for *anything*, anything at *all* that could go wrong."

Gertie silently read it over and then she read it out loud. "No. I don't see any problems at all."

I didn't either, but it pays to have a proofreader. "Good. Then I guess we'll just see how well it works out!" With that, Gertie and I got ready for the cookout at Lindsey's. Hunter finally called and he gladly offered to pick Gertie and me up on his way. Just before it was time for Hunter to arrive, Luna stepped out of the hallway, carrying a little scroll of paper in her mouth. She jumped up on my desk and dropped it.

"Now what?" I said as I picked up the little scroll of parchment. It had a wax seal that said Witches Union Local 1313, and it was addressed to Gertie.

"Thank you, Luna." She bent down and gave her a kiss on the head. Gertie unrolled the scroll, which inexplicably seemed to grow much longer than the little rolled up piece of paper she started with. "Wow."

"Wow what? What is it, Gertie?"

"It seems they have sent a list of certain characters they expect to have in your book, as well as what I assume is a basic plot they expect you to follow. Including how it ends."

She handed me the scroll and I read through it. "Are you kidding me? And did you read this note on the bottom? There's a deadline. Two weeks from today they will be expecting a completed manuscript."

"I saw that, too. Do you think you'll be able to write it by then?"

"In their dreams! They can all just get in line to kiss my ass. This story was my idea to do, anyway. To be honest, I don't even know if I feel like writing it anymore. What's the worst that could happen if I don't have it done and the way they want it written?"

"No! No, no, no, no, NO! You don't understand. Those old witches don't just make suggestions. They issue commands. And the worst that could happen? Need I remind you what an angry old witch can do? And those witches are old and they are always ready to flip into all out bitch mode at the drop of a hat. You'll have to do it, and I'll help you any way that I can."

"Well, we can talk about it later. Hunter should be here any minute. I'm not letting this bother me today. Not yet."

Chapter Fifteen
An Enchanted Afternoon

As promised, Hunter arrived and the three of us traveled over to Lindsey's. Kelly was already there, and she had brought along two of her little nephews. I sometimes had a hard time keeping the progeny of Kelly's siblings straight. She was the youngest of seven children, and her three sisters and two of her brothers were now all married with children. When I say children, I mean they were the offspring of Satan and his evil concubines. Everyone lived in close proximity to each other, and the children seemed to be completely interchangeable among families. The last time I was able to get a full count, Lucifer had managed to procreate sixteen times. Although there were at least two sets of twins in the mix. That was certainly a cruel joke to make it more difficult for people like me.

Kelly's single brother, Randy, had arrived at the cookout and Gertie became very excited when she saw him. I remembered there were still a couple of things that I needed to talk to Gertie about concerning Randy. For the moment, I was occupied with defending myself from the onslaught of a demon attack brought on by Kelly's twin six year old nephews. Gertie skipped across the lawn and shouted out, "Hey! Randy! Randy Johnson!"

"Oh. My God. She didn't just say that out loud." Lindsey threw her hand over her mouth.

"I believe she did. I don't think she knows the whole story." Kelly added.

"Let me talk to her when I get the chance." I just had to wait for the opportunity. The sooner the better it would be.

Now I have a problem I know many other elementary school teachers have as well. It seems we can all agree, within the confines of the classroom or even the playground, we are able to tame even the worst of the little ogres. If you should take everyone outside of school and put them in a family gathering, we suddenly become nearly powerless. It should be surprising, but in fact we are used to it. Even with three elementary school educators present with all of our combined experience and training, we may as well be trying to tame some of Gertie's paranormal beasts. Still, I envied Kelly's big and boisterous family, the one she always referred to as a "mixed" family. To her a mixed multicultural family was part Italian and part Jewish Russian.

The real surprise occurred when Luke and Derek showed up. At least Hunter and I were quite surprised. Before long they had paired up with Kelly and Lindsey. Lindsey winked at me and gave me a thumbs up in gratitude for fixing the issue. I was pretty well planted in one place with the weight of a baby demon hanging on each leg. Thankfully, Hunter pried the vermin away and took them to play with a ball he spied lying in the grass. I saw Gertie temporarily break away from Randy and I seized the opportunity to give her a fair warning.

"Gertie, I need to talk to you about something. It's about Randy."

"Oh! Isn't he just the sweetest? He always dresses so well and he is just so outgoing and funny."

"Exactly. Have you noticed his well-manicured nails? And was his friend Mark with him last night?"

"Those guys were pretty drunk last night. They were so funny. You should have seen them goofing around and grabbing at each other. They were hilarious."

"Okay, first, Randy's last name is not Johnson. That's more of a—nickname that I suppose his friend Mark gave him. And before you get your romantic little heart set on Randy, you need to know that he is gay."

"Oh, isn't it great? That is exactly what he said. That he was gay. I told him I'm gay, too. I think everyone should be gay. He asked something about me, kind of strange. Somehow or another he must have found out about how I accidentally appeared in your coat closet. I don't recall what he said exactly, but he asked me how long I'd been out. I had no idea what he meant and then he said that he meant out of the closet, how long have I been out of the closet. So, obviously he knew about that. I told him you were the one to help get me out of the closet and that you were my special friend. I even told him I was spending the weekend with you at your place."

"You didn't! What did Randy say?"

"He said that it explains a lot about you! That he never sees you with a guy. But that must have been the alcohol talking, because it didn't make a lick of sense to me."

I looked up and saw Randy give me a smile and a little wave and nod from across the yard. The problem here was that Randy and I knew each other for many years. I completely embarrassed myself with him when I was in high school. I literally threw myself at him and he rejected me. The thing was, at that time, Randy hadn't figured out what was going on with himself, so he never told me why he rejected me. For the longest time I thought he despised me. It took a while until the awkwardness finally wore off.

"Gertie, what I'm trying to say here is that Randy isn't attracted to girls. He likes boys. Mark is his boyfriend. And the word *gay* nowadays means somebody that is attracted to a person of the same sex. Does this make any sense? I have to add that it is perfectly acceptable for people to feel that way and live that way. Just saying that since I know you are from an entirely different time when it may not have been."

"Oh. Oh! I get it. Yeah, that kind of thing happened then, too. It just wasn't talked about outside of certain circles, of course. Now I know what Mark meant when I said everyone should be as gay as us. He said that at least there would be a lot more bars to hang out in."

"Just be his friend. He's a nice guy. Remember though, you're only going to be good friends. That's all. And that's okay."

"All right. Just my luck. Well, I'll just have to keep my eyes open. There's plenty of fish in the sea!" Gertie shrugged off her disappointment in her usual bubbly fashion and went back to Randy. I thought about what she said and looked at Hunter, who was busy kicking a ball around with the little twins. *I don't know about the other fish in the sea. I don't see myself throwing this one back in. Ever.*

The afternoon went by wonderfully. Everyone mingled and mixed, Lindsey's grilling was incredible. We were all relaxing on the patio, talking and listening to the radio, then something happened that made all of us ladies freeze solid, each with completely shocked faces. The DJ provided us with a news update.

"Some pretty bizarre news today from Arlington International Racetrack. There was some excitement when an apparent prankster replaced two of the thoroughbreds with, now get this, a unicorn and another with Pegasus! That's right, a one-horned unicorn and the winged horse of ancient Greek mythology, Pegasus!

Perplexed officials have actually described the animals as a mythical unicorn and the other as Pegasus. Now don't be too alarmed. I'm sure it was just a horse with some sort of a fake horn somehow strapped on its head like a party hat. The other with a set of corny foam wings. My guess is that this is some sort of publicity stunt, but I, for one, am not buying it."

I finally wiggled my index finger and motioned for the girls to pull closer to me. "We've got to talk about this. Meet me in the kitchen."

Once Gertie, Kelly, and Lindsey filed in through the back door, we gathered around the island heaped with half empty serving bowls of various sides and salads. "I don't even remember seeing a third of these today." Kelly observed. She then swept her finger through another bowl that had the remains of chocolate frosting. "You did? You made your chocogasm cake? Where is it? Bring it on before all the men get their paws on it!"

"In time, Kelly. In time. Why rush it? I want to make sure everyone has a chance to settle down from everything else."

"Food foreplay before chocogasm. Sounds ideal." I brought everyone down a notch and said, "Well, what the hell do we do now? A unicorn and a flying horse? Anyone?"

"I can't change them back. I don't know how. I just hope that the union doesn't find out about this. They really frown upon public displays of magic, at least as extravagant as putting mythical creatures in a horserace—and with my record—I hate to think of what they would do."

"That's another thing. As long as they had them there, why didn't they just race them? Imagine the publicity mileage they could have gotten out of that?" Lindsey remarked with complete sincerity.

"I say we don't do a thing. Deny, deny, de—" Kelly was interrupted by a loud crack and a puff of black smoke.

Chapter Sixteen
Let's Go, Witches

"All right, witches. Who was the comedian at the horse track?" It was none other than Esmeralda. She had swapped her many-sizes-too-small business suit for black leather pants and a black leather bodice trimmed with darkened gold and blood red paisley panels. All of it was so tight, she looked as if it may have been painted on. Her hair was wildly let down, it had curls, and it was big. She finished off the look with high heeled, black leather boots.

Lindsey didn't faint this time when a witch appeared of out thin air. "Would it hurt for you people to knock or something? It's more than a little unnerving to have a paranormal dominatrix just pop up in your kitchen."

"Dominatrix," Esmeralda said slowly in a low tone. "Dominatrix," she said again as she walked closer to Lindsey. She eyed up Lindsey, feeling her hair. "Well, well. If that's what comes to mind, you know what that means?"

Lindsey shook her head.

"It means, Dorothy, I get to be the wicked witch that finally gets to inflict some punishment on a very naughty farm girl."

"Huh?" Lindsey really was the poor naïve farm girl and it took her a few minutes to grasp what Esmeralda had said. "Oh!"

I silently agreed with Lindsey. I thought to myself, *all you need is a riding crop. You would make a textbook dominatrix.*

Esmeralda snapped her head towards me and looked me over. "Oh, I have one, sweetie. Maybe next time I'll bring it along and you two can be my witches for the night."

"Oh shit! Sorry. I forgot about the mindreading skills. And I'll pass on the whipping. Thank you."

"I'm going to cut to the chase. We have a little problem with a unicorn and a flying pony. The very problem that the union abhors. I'm willing to make it go away, but it'll cost you."

Kelly was still in self-preservation mode and she had no idea who she was addressing. "We? You have a mouse in your pocket? This sounds like a personal problem to me."

Esmeralda hissed at Kelly. She actually hissed. "Listen, I know it was one of these two buffoons." She pointed at Gertie and me. "And I'm guessing it had to be Miss O'Leary here. It would be just like a girl that farts rainbows to transform race horses into My Tiny Pony lookalikes."

Gertie was slightly upset. "Hey! I was drunk at the time!"

"Oh, that will definitely be a great excuse." The sarcasm dripped from Esmeralda.

"Did they really turn out looking like My Tiny Pony toys?" Lindsey asked.

"Yes, in all of their fucked up rainbow and butterfly glory. Like I said, this goes away under one condition. You two witches are going to help me out. As much as it nauseates me to say this, I need allies. Unfortunately, you two are the only ones I can trust—or blackmail if you prefer that."

"What do you mean? What is it that you need us to do?"

"The old bitches on the union board have a plot. They want to take control of everything supernatural. And there are all sorts of supernaturals out there that they have never told you about. One dangerous type that no longer exists are the vampires. Not for a hundred years. Even before that, they were very rare. I don't miss them at all. They were nothing but a bunch of moody crybabies and drama queens if you ask me."

"Why were they so dangerous then?"

"They were the only supernaturals that had the ability to kill other supernaturals. They weren't invincible of course. You could take them out with a fucking toothpick, they were afraid of garlic, they couldn't be in the light. They had more rules than you could count. Still, they were feared by everyone, including mortals. It is because of them that the Yetis vanished just for their fur. Unicorns? Vampires feasted on them. Dragons, history. Mermaids? Nearly wiped out, and they are just now making a comeback. Smelly bitches. I could go on. Anyway, the union wants a vampire. A very powerful vampire that they can create and control. The only way to do it is through the use of the very rare *literal magic* that you have stumbled upon, Leigh. And, Gertie, as much as I dislike everything about your wardrobe and your disgustingly happy personality, you are the only witch with the ability to recreate supernatural creatures that have been extinct for centuries. The union wants those creatures back, and they want to be the supreme leaders of all supernatural creatures. Their plan is to have you, Leigh, write what they want to happen and they want to maintain control through fear. Fear of their very own powerful vampire. I don't know about you, but I have no desire to be under their thumbs."

"So, why don't I just refuse to do what they want?"

"They will make you, Leigh. You have no idea what and who they will go after to make you write what they want. This is where we have to work together. I plan to take over the board. I'm going to be the Chair and you two the other officers. It will take very careful and very secret planning. I'll be listening in to all of their plans, and I will go over every piece of your story as you move along. Those witches won't know what hit them."

From her expression, Gertie must have thought Esmeralda had completely lost her mind. "Take control of the union? What are you thinking? You know how old and powerful those witches are."

"Listen, Sunshine, don't doubt me. None of you witches better doubt me. I'm an original, old school badass. Straight outta Salem."

"Ooh, gangsta witch!" Kelly laughed. "Listen, I applaud you for trying to bring in the gangster attitude, but it doesn't mix at all with your sophisticated, condescending, and sardonic alpha bitch shtick."

Esmeralda gave Kelly a scathing look as a response. "Enough of this! I'm here for Leigh and Gertie. They've got what I want and need."

Just then Randy walked into the kitchen, and it was obvious he caught the last thing Esmeralda said. He took one look at Esmeralda and then he looked at me. "Well, well, I am just learning all sorts of new things today." Randy smiled at me and then looked at Esmeralda. In his typical over-the-top expressive tone he said, "*Love* the look. We need to shop—"

Esmeralda snapped her fingers and Randy was instantly frozen. Literally, he was frozen with ice and frost. "Holy snowballs! I need to learn how to do that!"

Kelly said. She tapped on her brother's frozen head. "Nice work!"

Lindsey was equally impressed. "No kidding! You have no idea how often I would be using that on people. I would actually look forward to having to deal with jackasses and morons just so I could abracadabra their stupid asses into ice sculptures." I knew Lindsey was dead serious when she said that. After all, who *wouldn't* want to be able to do that?

"Well, speaking for those who have been frozen, it is not an entirely fun experience. I wouldn't want to use it on people." Gertie was untypically somber. "Well, not very often." Gertie giggled. "Anyway, that's Kelly's brother, Randy, would you please thaw him out?"

"Oh, don't worry, when we're done. Now back to what—"

I was still laughing about what Lindsey had said, and I imagined how often I would be freezing people throughout the course of my day. Kelly suddenly reminded everyone of what she had been waiting for. "Hey! Enough of the foreplay, let's have a chocogasm!"

"Oh, and speaking of that, tell us all about what happened last night. Did you have multiple Hunter-gasms!" Lindsey was laughing at her own little joke.

"Oh, yes, do tell us about it. From what I figured out, Gertie must have been passed out in your bathroom while you were getting your head slammed against the headboard."

Gertie looked at me, half shocked and half amused. Her squeaky innocent voice made it worse. "Really, Leigh? You were? While I was lying there all drunk and cold in your tub? I thought I heard something. I didn't know what it meant. I thought you had stubbed your toe because the day I left with the girls you busted your toe on a chair and yelled out, 'Fuck me!' But *last night* I heard you say it just a little different. You said: 'Fuck me! Please just fuck me! Fuck me! Oh, yes, baby!'

"Hey, I had been waiting for an opportunity with Hunter. There was no way in hell that I was going to blow it with him."

Kelly put the chocolate frosting covered spoon to her lips and sensually licked it. "Really, Leigh, I'm willing to bet my next paycheck that you in fact are going to *blow it.*"

Now they were in tears and roaring with laughter at my expense, that is everyone but Esmeralda.

"Hell, yeah, I'd—" Lindsey started to say something to add to my public humiliation.

"Enough!" Esmeralda's voice boomed so loud that it made us all jump. "What the fuck is wrong with you women? Are you *all* off of your medications? Can't you stay on one fucking topic? I came here to talk to you about some serious shit. And you are acting like it's the waiting room at an ADHD clinic. Here's the deal. I took away the fluffy pink unicorn with a rainbow mane and the purple horse with butterfly wings."

I looked at Kelly and tried not to laugh. Kelly made a comically snooty face and whispered, "Serious shit and fluffy, too." We lost it and were laughing again.

"Damn you! I'm ready to freeze the lot of you. Gertie's creations are now safe and sound at her home for wayward cats." She pointed at Gertie and then at me. "You two are my witches now. You go ahead and start writing that story, Leigh. And pronto. Gertie, refrain from creating any more monstrosities, and wait until it's time to create exactly what supernaturals we'll need and when."

"So, I *will* be resurrecting Vlad the hybrid in my book?"

"Oh yes, you will, but there will be a twist the union won't know about, and I'll disclose that to you in due time. I do have a plan, and to give you a hint at what I am going for, just think of the story of the Trojan horse."

"I guess we don't have much of a choice. I have to tell you that if this works out like you are planning, I won't be able to offer any time whatsoever to a union position once school starts back up."

"Don't worry about that. You'll only need to cast an annual vote at most. I'll handle everything else." Just as Esmeralda finished speaking, Kelly's nephews charged in through the door and latched onto her legs. "Oh, Gertie, now what did you come up with?" She looked down and scowled. "Elves on crack. Nice. First one to start humping my leg gets incinerated."

Kelly barked at Esmeralda, "Hey! Those are my little nephews you're talking about, witch. You could try being nice."

"Oh, this is as nice as I get, doll. Little twin humans, elves on crack, same thing." With a snap of her fingers and a puff of smoke, she was gone as quick as she came, and Randy was instantly returned to his old self.

"Hey, what just happened? I could have sworn I was talking to some leather clad woman standing right there."

Kelly guided her brother back out the door. "You've had too much sun. Go sit down in the shade for a bit."

Chapter Seventeen
Hot, So Hot

"Well, that was really unexpected. What do you think, Gertie? Do we trust that Esmeralda is telling the truth?" Personally, I had my doubts.

"Everything that Esmeralda said matches up with the stories I've heard about vampires and supernatural creatures. I don't doubt the union is out to take control of everything and everyone. If she told us the truth, I would have to agree with her that the witches running the union need to be replaced."

In my mind, Gertie was right. I still had reservations about how far we could trust Esmeralda. I looked at Lindsey and Kelly to see if they were going to weigh in on the issue.

Lindsey held her hands up. "Don't look at me. I'm not a witch, and I'm still trying to figure out why any witch would be in trouble for creating magical creatures out of racehorses. As for Esmeralda, she is pretty abrasive and about as welcome here as a porcupine at a nudist colony." Lindsey's country upbringing always had a way of coming out.

"I can answer that," Gertie replied. "The witches that run the union are very old. They've survived a lot of witch hunts over the centuries. They know that the best way to avoid persecution is to keep a low profile. And they want to be in control of everything. It makes sense to do that, I suppose, but the fact is that they aren't interested in anyone else's well-being, like a real union should be. They are all about power and preserving themselves. Witches like Leigh and me are a liability to them, the only reason they tolerate us is because they need our unique powers."

I was curious to know what Kelly thought. "Kelly, what do you think about this whole thing?"

"I wouldn't trust her completely, but I would side with her, cautiously. It sounds like you can't trust the union bosses either. If I had to pick between the two, I would side with Esmeralda. She came to you two with this and that means she trusts you not to say anything to the union. Her actions prove that much. Anyway, like Lindsey said, I'm not a witch, so I'm really not involved."

"We are all best friends. You may not be involved, but I really value both of your opinions. And unfortunately based on how things have been working out so far, you're both liable to get dragged in at some point. Sorry." I was genuinely and truly sorry.

"Why don't we take out the cake and everyone get in on some chocogasm. I'm sure Leigh would like to get some time in with Hunter. I know Kelly and I are hoping to spend a little quality time with Luke and Derek. And, Gertie—well, I don't know what to say, but you ought to hang out with Kelly and I, and the boys. One good look at you and I am pretty sure they can rustle up a single friend. What do you say?"

"I say hell yes!" Gertie was looking well beyond Randy now, who was off to pick up his friend from work.

Our cookout came to an end after a delicious chocogasm. This time I wasn't too worried about Gertie getting into any mischief with the girls. It seemed that for the moment, barring any more surprises from Esmeralda, things were calm. No crazed gorillas, no fluffy mythical beasts, no leather and lace dom, nothing at all to cause witchy chaos. It was going to be a great night.

Hunter and I rode back to my place, and it goes without saying what happened as soon as we got in the door. Well, technically things started happening on the ride back, but I'm talking about a ripping each other's clothes off kind of thing. As a matter of fact, it was right when the clothes ripping phase was completed when I got a call from Lindsey. Of course, I could tell that Kelly squeezed her face in next to Lindsey's in order to be part of the conversation. They spoke in hushed and saddened voices, and in annoying alternating sentences. I couldn't get a word in for a while.

"Hi, Leigh? It's about Gertie."

"Luke and Derek don't have any single friends around here!"

"Yeah, Gertie looks completely bummed out."

"Isn't she? I know. It is so unlike her."

"We were hoping you could ask Hunter if he knows anyone. If not, we'll send Luke and Derek away and just have a girl's night, but we'd rather not have to."

Finally they both stopped talking. I was able to quickly say three words, "Let me check." I gave Hunter a brief rundown on the situation and he didn't know any guys that were available and local. This was one of those times for me when I knew exactly what I'd end up doing, even though I knew damn well that it was against my own best judgment. While the girls continued chatting about something that I had completely tuned out, I quickly excused myself from Hunter. Of course, I went to right to my desk. The thought of Gertie feeling heartbroken and alone was too much to bear. I had to think fast and think straight. It didn't have to be good, it just had to sort of fit into the story.

The young and beautiful witch, who was always so happy and upbeat, was beginning to feel a little lonely. Lonely for a romantic companion. A man that was worthy of her affection. It was quite by coincidence that night, as her friends were courted by their men, that a man of such caliber crossed her path.

Hunter! It was all I could think about just then. He was still lying in my bed, naked and waiting. *Think, Leigh! Think!* What would Gertie like? I wasn't even sure what she preferred. She certainly was impressed by the sight of Hunter when he stumbled in on us. *She likes hot and masculine. Good, stereotype hotties—Hmm, I bet a fireman. She can meet a hot as hell fireman, and I'll let them take it from there.* "Got it!" I said out loud.

"What's that, babe?" Hunter had heard me.

"Oh, I just found something I was looking for! Be right there."

The man that came to light her flame was a young, smoking hot fireman. He had a body that was sculpted as if he were a Greek God. Smart, funny, and kind were his best personality traits. He spied the young witch and was drawn to her. From that point on, her night would no longer be dull and boring.

"Good enough." I got up from my desk and was ready to sprint to the bedroom when I remembered I told Hunter I had found what I was looking for. *What the hell would I have been looking for? Think, think, think.*

"Hey, babe, you need any help?"

"No. On my way!" I went into the hallway and as I passed the bathroom I grabbed something off of the counter. I wasn't even sure what it was. I only wanted a prop. I looked in my hand as I reached the bedroom. I had grabbed the goddamn toothbrush holder. I bounded across the floor and jumped into the bed while I simultaneously tossed the toothbrush holder onto my dresser.

"I'm curious. What did you bring back?" Really? He just asked me that?

"Just freshening my mouth a bit." Then I did exactly what any woman would do when she wanted her man to drop the topic. I went down on him. The blowjob, as it turns out, can be a very powerful item in a woman's arsenal. You can make a man forget what he was talking about. You can motivate him to do any number of favors. If you think that is being manipulative, you are damn right.

I had never experienced an all-nighter. Maybe it wasn't all night, but we had sex in more ways than I thought were possible, and the time was measured in hours not minutes. At some point we just collapsed on each other. I looked at Hunter and in a sleepy voice I asked him, "You're staying here with me tonight, aren't you?"

"I wouldn't want to be anywhere else."

If I hadn't already told myself, I was falling in love. Now I definitely acknowledged the fact that I had plunged smack down into it. I laid my head on his chest and shut my eyes for all of two minutes. My phone was ringing from somewhere in the apartment. Luna jumped up on the bed and joined me on Hunter's chest.

"Meow, meow."

"Okay, I want to ignore the phone, but Luna seems to be trying to tell me something. I better find it." I reluctantly got up and hunted down my phone. The phone was laying on the living room floor, next to a heap of our clothes. I looked at the missed calls. There were over a dozen from Lindsey and Kelly. *Oh shit, what did I do now?*

That question was quickly answered once I called Kelly.

"Did you practice a little witchcraft tonight?"

I winced. Physically I winced, and I held the phone away from my ear at Kelly's scathing tone.

"Yes." I said very sheepishly. "What happened?"

"Let me guess, you decided to set Gertie up with a hot fireman? You do know that a hot fireman is not going to show up unless there is a goddamn fucking FIRE!"

"Oh. No. How bad?"

"Leigh, what were you thinking?" Kelly's voice had softened. "Shortly after we talked to you about Gertie, we all went into the house to hang out for a bit. At some point, Gertie got up and went back out to the patio. Just when I thought about going out to check on her, she came charging into the living room, babbling almost incoherently. Apparently, Lindsey had left the gas grill on and she also had left food on the rack. Gertie must have noticed that there was a lot of smoke coming out of it, and she opened it up to check it out. She has a very serious issue with fire. Did you know that? She completely lost it."

"Yeah, I can just imagine."

"Well, when she opened it, kaboom! All the grease, from whatever poor creature Lindsey forgot in there, burst into flames. Gertie panicked. She didn't know anything about how a gas grill works. Otherwise, she would have just shut the lid and turned off the gas. So she took the long metal tongs that Lindsey had hanging there and she grabbed the mass of flaming fat. She tried to yank it off the grill. I have no idea what she thought she was going to do with it, but in any case, she pulled it off and it went flying over her shoulder, right through Lindsey's open kitchen window. That shit hit the curtains and the walls like it was a fucking napalm bomb."

"Are you guys all okay?"

"Yes, shook up, but okay. I don't know who called the fire department, but I'm glad they came when they did. It seemed like half of the house was in flames. Lindsey got it the worst. She grabbed a fire extinguisher and tried like hell to put it out, but it wasn't enough. Poor Lindsey was coughing so bad it worried me. Suddenly, this absolutely drop dead gorgeous hunk of fireman stomps down the door. Does he rush to Lindsey who is obviously struggling from the smoke? No, he runs right over to Gertie, scoops her up in his arms and runs outside with her. I would have thought that he would have rushed right back in, but he didn't. Some other firemen came in and grabbed her. When we got out to the front lawn, there's the hot fireman peeling off his firefighting suit. He and Gertie were all over each other. It was damn near a public sex show. Lindsey is fine. She is staying with me for now until her place gets cleaned up. Luke and Derek were fun until the fire pretty much ended the evening for us and they left shortly after."

"So, where is Gertie now?"

"My guess is that she is still playing with her new toy somewhere."

"Really? Sweet, tiny, little Gertie?"

"You didn't see this guy, Leigh. He was smoking hot, literally. You could see the steam coming off of his bare chest when they were on the front lawn. Apparently your magic spell was at full power for them both."

"Call when you hear from her. I'll be waiting for her, too. I sure hope she is okay."

"Don't worry too much, she seemed like she had a pretty good idea of what she wanted. I bet she is still making up for all of those lost years."

I looked at the clock. Four in the morning. I was exhausted and I slowly walked back down the hallway to crawl in bed. There was a muffled sound and just a little pink smoke coming from behind me. Gertie had made it back.

"That was horrible! Just horrible!" She said as she laid back on the couch.

"I am so glad you're back safe and sound! I heard about the fire. Where did you go?"

"The hospital. First, I just want to say that I am pretty sure this was one of your spells, but don't worry, I appreciate the thought."

"Ugh. I really had no idea. I just wanted you to have a little romantic run-in with a super hot fireman."

"You sure got it right! When we saw each other, he just snatched me up and took me outside. It was so exciting. I thought he was going to completely ravish me right there on the front lawn. He was super hot, just like you hoped for. As a matter of fact, he started to feel so hot, he felt like he was burning up in his firefighting ensemble. He quickly stripped it off. Then I started to feel like I was on fire inside. Like someone lit a fire inside of me."

I cringed. "That would be about right. I believe I wrote that he would light a flame inside of you."

"Don't worry. One of the other nice firemen called for an ambulance, and we got to ride together to the hospital. Even though we were sweating and nearly passing out from the heat, he kissed me. He kissed me like crazy. I've never had a kiss like that. *Andddd* I've never had a man touch me the way he was touching me. I could barely handle it. If it wasn't for the heat exhaustion getting in the way and that annoying IV, I may have actually done it with him. We got to the hospital and I didn't get to see him again for a couple of hours. It seemed like once we were separated, we both got back to our old selves. Thank God that when they let us both out, the heat between us was turned down to a fun sizzling feeling. I don't do well with charbroiled."

"So it worked out in the end, after all? I mean, other than the fact that Lindsey's kitchen looks like someone took a flamethrower to it and you two were hospitalized for heat exhaustion. Seriously, did I forget anything?"

Gertie started to laugh about it. "He took me out to breakfast and I got his number. His name is Brad. Oh, Leigh, I don't even know what to say. He really is a sweet guy, but what I really like is the fact that he makes me feel like I'm standing in front of a buffet of delicious food. And I don't even know where to start, which is a little problem. Guys, dating, romance, and especially sex, it's all new to me. Back in the 1870s I was probably on my way to spinsterhood. I was a seamstress and housekeeper from the poorest of Irish immigrants. Actually, I was getting too old to still be single. Now here I am in this wonderful world, but as far as being a woman, if you know what I mean by that, in this day—I've got a lot to learn about it."

"I think it's sweet and so are you Gertie. Don't worry, we'll help you out with every bit of advice we've been given. The same advice that has failed us time and again!"

Chapter Eighteen
Time for Me to Fly

It was almost noon on Sunday when I woke up. Hunter got up and after a bit headed to the shower. It gave me a minute to think. Although, that's probably the worst thing a person can do early on in a hot and heavy relationship. My heart was going full steam ahead and it could care less what my brain was saying. It was giving it the finger as it zipped passed it, shouting at it to get out of the way, completely ignoring all caution signs and exits along the way. Heartbreak Drive Exit 42, Rejection Road Exit 45, Surprise Baggage Boulevard Exit 60, Unplanned Pregnancy Exit 80, Happily Ever After Avenue Exit 100.

Did I need to step back a bit and figure out where I thought this was all going? Did I have expectations of something permanent? I hadn't discussed it with Hunter. How do you do that anyway? I've only just met the guy this summer. *Do I just straight out ask him? Oh, Hunter, I have something to ask you. Do you see us getting married at some point, preferably earlier than later? How about children? I want more than one, how about you? What do you think of big weddings by the way?* Talk about scaring someone off. Hell, I was scaring myself off.

I should have probably put out some sort of expectations for Hunter, so that he at least knew I wasn't just doing this for the great sex before I threw my heart out in the air like it was a Frisbee. Well, yes, I was doing it for the great sex. I was also hoping for so much more, and all the signs seemed to be pointing that I had every reason to be hopeful. I already learned something,

something that made me sit back and sip on my tea and feel wise: *Sometimes it is easier to hang onto the hope that your assumptions were right. You assume he feels the same way you do.* Then I heard the voice of my Dad. *You know what they say when you assume something, Leigh? It makes an ass out of you and me.* I found myself talking out loud. "I've heard you say that a million times, Dad." Rather than just ask Hunter about where we were and where we might be going with *us*, I went with my assumptions.

Hunter stepped out of the shower and came out into the kitchen. He had nothing more on than a towel around his waist. *Great sex, that's just fine for me.* After he leaned down to kiss me, all of my earlier worries faded away. He walked behind me and massaged my shoulders, occasionally stopping to nibble on my neck and ears. Slowly, he came around to my side and the towel dropped to his feet. Hunter was now a naughty tease.

"Shoot! You don't know this, but Gertie came in this morn—" Just then Gertie walked into the kitchen.

Hunter simply froze, unable to decide what to do. Gertie's eyes were instantly transformed from sleepy, squinting crevices to huge round glassy pools. And they were fixated on Hunter's throbbing, jumbo-sized erection. "Sweet Mother of God! I had no idea!"

Hunter scooped up the towel and hastily threw it around himself, then he made a dash for the bedroom.

Gertie started to laugh. "Holy cow! Doesn't that thing hurt you? I've never seen a man's hard one before. Oh, sweet baby Jesus!"

"Oh God, Gertie, I'm sorry. I forgot Hunter didn't know you were here. I didn't know he was going to take the towel off." I paused and thought about what she had said. "Are you being serious? You've never—seriously? I mean, you had to have caught a quick peek at some point? Right?"

"No! I told you, I have a lot to learn about. A lot!"

Hunter was walking towards the door and he was fully clothed. "I just want to grab my mail. I picked it up yesterday and left it in my truck. I forgot all about it."

A minute later he returned to the kitchen and smiled at Gertie. She blushed and became more giddy than usual. I gave her a nudge with my elbow. The always honest and free speaking Gertie told us what had her spun up. "I'm sorry, but when I look at you now, all I get is that image of you naked and your big penis pointing up." Hunter immediately sat down, concealing the part of him below the waist.

"This could be a little awkward now." Hunter said as he looked through his mail. Luna jumped up on the table and she was slapping the letters with one paw. Hunter stopped to look at one of the letters, then quickly ripped it open. "It's from the Chicago Police Academy Office. I applied for a special program they have for recently discharged military police. They are running a special short tracked academy program. A pilot program that I've heard about in other cities, and now Chicago is giving it a try. I had sent copies of all of my military service records and qualifications in to them, and they say here that I've been accepted!"

"What does that mean for you? I mean, your schedule?"

"It means I will be a fulltime city police officer a lot quicker than the six month academy I was planning to attend." Hunter looked at me and his smile fell a little.

"That's great! Isn't it? You look like you're not so sure."

"I have to report this week. I have to go and get a full physical tomorrow and I'll be pretty well locked into training for four weeks. I have been planning to ask you if you wanted to take off for a few days. Introduce you to my parents here in Chicago and then take a trip up to Minnesota for a few days for some camping. While we were up there, I wanted to visit my sister and her husband, and my nieces and nephews of course. You could get to meet them, and I know they would really like you."

My mouth nearly hit the floor. Gertie nailed me in the thigh with her knee and then whispered to in my ear, "His parents, his sister all the way in Minnesota? I'd say it's safe to say that he is planning for a future with you!"

"Shush." I whispered back. Then I responded to Hunter. "That would be awesome! If you still want to plan it when it's a better time, you can count me in!"

We all had lunch together and chatted some more, then the time came for Hunter to be on his way. Gertie said she needed to get home, but after an exciting weekend she was reluctant to leave. "I've just had so much fun being here with you, Kelly, and Lindsey. I don't have a choice, really. I have to be going back." Gertie looked around the room and I could tell she was thinking of an idea. "Hey! How about if you come with me for a few days? You can bring Luna. You can meet my cats, and of course you can see what I've been doing with the paranormal pet shop."

"It sounds great! But—I do have to work on that damn *Four-Bitten Fangtasy*, which by the way scares the daylights out of me, because I have no idea what the fallout will be for anyone around me."

"It'll be fine. If you come with me, I'll help you come up with the storyline. We'll even make up all of the names you will be using from scratch. They will be complete gibberish. Nobody will have those names. Perfectly safe. Hunter is going to be busy anyway. Come on, what do you say?" She waited a bit and then tempted me, "I'll show you around New Orleans! All of the best writers come to New Orleans! Some even live there." She skipped across my kitchen floor. "And—there is so much I still need to tell you about being a witch, and I have so many questions for you about how to be a modern woman!"

"How can I resist?" After all, Hunter was going to be busy. Lindsey was going to be dealing with her insurance company and getting a major remodeling project set up. Kelly would be at her wits end with having Lindsey for a roommate, and I'm certain she would flip her bitch switch in less than a day of that.

Gertie threw her arms open and was charging to hug me. Luna launched herself from the table right into Gertie's chest, and before I knew it, we were all locked in a three-way hug. I eventually wiggled free, packed a bag with some clothes and essentials, and I was ready.

"Dang it! We never performed that ceremony! You know, to present you with your official witch's broom."

"Don't worry about it, Gertie. No need to stress out over it. After all, the thing is so tiny. When you whipped it out, and I saw how small it was—well, it was very anticlimactic. Been there, done that before!" I laughed at my *little* joke, but Gertie looked at me like I had just spoken in Swahili.

"I don't get what you mean."

"Never mind. Let's go!" We both held our little brooms up while Gertie carefully recited the spell. We all poofed away to Louisiana, little brooms still in hand.

Chapter Nineteen
Welcome to The Pussy Plantation

Gertie, Luna, and I instantly arrived at the end of a long, neglected dirt road. The view was stereotypical of any bayou country horror flick. Live oaks with sad long locks of Spanish moss seemed to be solemn witnesses to our arrival as we began the long walk through the afternoon shadows towards Gertie's place. I saw a hand-painted sign. A rectangular piece of plywood that had been painted pink. Neatly made purple lettering spelled out *Gertie's Pussy Plantation.*

Luna seemed to be at unease among the overgrown open spaces. She made little crying sounds as we walked. "Come here, city cat." I bent down and Luna jumped into my arms. "Gertie, I don't know what to say. This is definitely not like any place I could picture you living in."

"I'm sorry. I haven't gotten around to this part of the property. I had to concentrate on the house first, then the area around it, along with the out buildings. I was able to use some magic, but I'm no expert like Esmeralda is. I have to remember to change that sign back there, too. Cheer up you two, it brightens up a bit as we get closer!"

"Why did you have us teleport so far down the road anyway?"

"To be dramatic. Spooky, isn't it?" Gertie gave me a sly look. "Just kidding! If you haven't noticed, I tend to end up not quite where I need to be. In a big and very old house that has had a lot of changes made to it—well, let's just say it can get kind of tricky. You might say your address and then exactly where you want to be and hope for the best. I once said kitchen and I ended up inside an old boarded up shed out back. To make things worse, it was already occupied by a family of cute little skunks. Even though I got sprayed and smelled like hell for weeks, they were very cute. Just adorable, really. Anyway, you see, when this place was built, they didn't have the kitchen in the house. It got way too hot to have cooking fires in the stoves and ovens inside, so they had a cookhouse out back. Apparently, these little brooms are very fussy. You don't even want to know what happened when I was in a rush to get home to use the bathroom."

"Oh yes, I do!"

"In an old abandoned latrine. I fell right through the rotten boards that covered a sludge filled hole, and I was up to my waist in it. It was a hundred times worse than getting skunked. I've found it to be worth the walk to just say my address. I always end up safely at the end of the drive."

"Why here? Why down in the bayou near New Orleans? You're a Chicago girl after all."

"Convenience I suppose. When I thawed out, I found myself at the witches union. So I was already in New Orleans. I had to listen to those witches jabber about the union, and the safety and security of all witches, blah, blah, blah—blah, blah. Once they were through, I just toured around. I wanted something in the country. After being frozen for a hundred years, I really had no desire to endure the winters in Chicago. Besides, I found a great way to make some money in a pinch. It's not exactly honest money, though. I probably shouldn't tell you."

"I'm dying to know! How dirty does it get?"

Gertie whispered as if she were making a jail cell confession to a murder, "Gambling." She looked around, worried that someone may have been listening and then her voice returned to normal. "Down in the French Quarter there is a casino. There are a few riverboat casinos in the area, also. I went to the one in the Quarter, and I saw a huge fortune wheel. I figured out a little spell that could make the wheel stop on exactly what number I wanted it to. The problem is that they only have one or two of those things set up at any given time. Eventually they tire of seeing me win over and over. They make up some excuse that I have to leave or offer me some free hotel nights or something. I tried the roulette tables, but that was useless, as were the dice games. I didn't try card games because I couldn't figure out a way to use a spell to win at that. It didn't matter, I also found a racetrack in Bossier City that has races for greyhounds, horses, and even harness racing. I probably got most of my money that way by making whatever animal I pick win the race."

"Don't feel too bad, those places have been cleaning out people's pockets for years. It's about time they get to see how it feels."

"I think I should be fine now for quite a while. I really don't want to go to Bossier City anymore. It is way over near Shreveport, which is in the complete opposite corner of the state from New Orleans. I don't know my way around there at all."

Suddenly I looked up and there it was, Gertie's Pussy Palace in all of its girly glory. It looked as if the paint scheme was created by a dozen sixth grade girls with instructions to use every single vivid color found in their packs of markers and crayons. The large front porch had a beautiful railing that wrapped around the front. Each spindle had a different color of paint. Each large porch column was colored like psychedelic candy sticks with every color in the rainbow twisting up the columns. I

128

could go on and on about the absolute detail to insanity. The décor sent a message. *The person that lives here is clearly nuts.* The bizarre paint job's assault on my eyesight was nearly matched by the equally splashy-colored, homemade lawn décor representing giant flowers and cute animals. Actually, there was no true lawn to speak of. Rather, it seemed to be surrounded by one giant flower bed and everything was in bloom.

"Oh look, Sherwin Williams threw up a house!" I was awestruck. "It's like looking through a fricking kaleidoscope. I expected it to be bright and cheery, but—wow! This place makes candy land look dull."

"Good! That is exactly the look I was going for. The *wow* look." Gertie looked off in the distance and shouted "Hi, babies! I'm back!" A cacophony of cat sounds replied an apparent welcome. "Don't worry, they don't all live in the house. Most of them live around the farm behind the house. There are two old barns and a number of smaller shelters for all of them."

"Don't you worry about getting them vaccinated and all that? That would be one hell of a veterinarian bill."

"Oh no, not a problem. Since every witch has to have a cat, there is a witch, which is the cat doctor." Gertie sometimes spoke at the speed of light.

"Stop right there, Gertie. My turn to be confused. So I heard that every witch has to have a cat. I got that much."

"Yup! So us witches have our very own cat doctor. She is a fellow witch, like us. Her name is Wanda."

"I suppose that I *mostly* understand now. Sorry. Please, go on."

"She is super nice, but a little wacky. You know how us cat ladies can be! She stops by once in a while and takes care of all of them. It only takes her a few minutes."

Luna and I followed Gertie into her house. All I could do was shake my head. Anything that a ten year old girl would scream about over its cuteness was in the house. It was completely and undeniably over the top. Gertie took us up to a spare bedroom so I could drop off my things, and then we went and sat in a room that she called the parlor.

"Beanbag chairs? Of course!"

"I know! Aren't they the most amazing thing? I had no idea that someone could have invented a chair so perfectly comfortable."

"Yes. They are fun. I can honestly say that I've never been in a room where the only chairs are beanbags. And each one is a different color of a neon rainbow." I looked around the room. "Or looked at a wall clock suspended by a gold painted chain from the neck of a giant plush toy giraffe. You are a trip, Gertie. A real trip."

"Like I've said, I grew up in a different time. A different world really. I was an orphan for as long as I can remember. All I know is that I was born in Ireland and I was raised by the Sisters at an orphanage in Chicago. We didn't have such a thing as a childhood back then, orphans or not. Only the very rich could have a luxury like that. The rest of us had to learn a trade and go to work. We didn't have toys. We didn't have bright colors. Now I can have all of those things. Everyone should have a childhood, everyone should have bright colors, and everyone should have a reason to smile. So that's me." Gertie lifted her hands up and looked around her room. "As for the cats, I see these poor creatures just left alone to fend for themselves and I know how they feel. I want to be able to give them a home and to know what it feels like to be loved."

"I think it's awesome. You're awesome, Gertie. Earlier you said that every witch needs a cat. Why is that?"

"According to Wanda, the witch-cat doctor, many cats are very old souls. The ones that were witches in a past life will always pair up with another witch. You may have noticed that Luna probably became very happy when you discovered that you're a witch. She gets to be the messenger and deliver your mail from other witches. She can help you in other ways, too, like letting you know where to find something that you've lost, or figure out something you don't understand. Some witches have said that their cats can use their own magic. I can't say that I've ever seen it personally, but I have no reason to doubt that certain *witch-cats* have that ability. As a matter of fact, when I was seventeen, a cat befriended me and she led me to a very old book of magic spells that was hidden in an attic of a church."

"Huh—" I thought about how Luna had transformed from demon cat to semi-affectionate feline. "I guess that's the reason for Luna's personality makeover ever since this all started. Are the witch-cats always black cats?"

"Always. I have never heard of any other type of cat belonging to a witch. Sorry, the stereotype is right on that at least."

"Oh, speaking of pets reminds me that I wanted to talk to you about something. You mentioned before about your idea for a Paranormal Pet Shop. I am really interested in that! Would you mind showing me what you've been concocting around here?"

"Are you sure, Leigh? Sometimes *even I* get a little shocked to see some of those critters."

I nodded my head that I was ready. Luna climbed up into my arms, apparently she was also cautiously ready to see what sorts of surprises Gertie had in store for us.

Chapter Twenty
The Paranormal Pet Shop

Gertie walked us through the rest of her huge Antebellum home, which of course was decorated as wildly as the parlor. Now I knew why Gertie surrounded herself with such bright colors for things both cute and beautiful. Actually, she didn't surround herself in it, she marinated herself in happiness and sunshine. I made up my mind then that I would follow her lead, but only enough to brighten my day now and again.

She took me to what had once been an entire separate wing of the mansion. I guessed that the master of the entire plantation had shared his house with a close relative's family. This part of the house had not been completely decorated yet. Rooms were recently painted in solid, bright colors, but the walls were bare. Apparently, Gertie had not yet collected enough cute, tacky, and downright gaudy, yet effeminate items to festoon the walls, doors, ceilings, and banisters.

"Welcome to my Paranormal Pet Shop!"

"Where? I was expecting stacked cages and pens. I thought it would be really noisy and a little smelly, just like an ordinary pet shop."

"Well, I don't believe in cages or pens. I just can't imprison any helpless creature. This is the main entrance room. I'm planning on painting murals on the walls of every type of magic animal that I've created. I am going to set up a really nice area where customers can have tea or coffee. Maybe cookies or something, but I'm not sure about leaving food out where the animals could get ahold of it."

We followed Gertie through a large door that opened to a sunny room with tall ceilings. The walls were painted a vivid yellow. There were double glass doors blocked wide open and I could see Gertie's wildflower yard waving in the breeze. "Here, take a look at this!" Gertie proudly exclaimed.

I looked around and didn't see anything at first. Just more of Gertie's big plush toys. I almost fainted when I saw they were alive. They were small fuzzy horses or horse like. There were six altogether. They stood about four feet tall, except for one that was only half the size of the others. Each had a different color of fur. They were cotton candy pink, light blue, lime-green, bright orange, purple, and the little one was bright red and had a white heart shape on its side. For a few seconds I worried that I had repeated my Denver incident by ingesting more magic brownies.

"Oh. My. God. Esmeralda was right about them. My Tiny Ponies brought to life. I see two unicorns, one with wings. It is just blowing my mind, Gertie."

"And to think that just a few weeks ago these were all abandoned Pit Bulls. I think they were once used for illegal dog fighting. They were just so aggressive and were hurting each other. Now look at them. Plus, they can come in here or go out and wander around the yard."

"What happened with the little one?"

"Oh, sorry. That happened to be a raccoon that mistakenly wandered into the barn where I had the dogs. I never saw him in there until he changed into that cute little thing. Just a happy accident. Now somewhere on the property are the ones that Esmeralda sent down here. I'm sure we'll come across them."

"Aren't you afraid that the one with wings will fly away?"

"No, I'm pretty sure they are more decorative than anything. He'll flutter them sometimes, but he can't get more than two feet off the ground and comes right back down again."

We left the fluffy little ponies to themselves and we went on to another room. This room was painted a tropical green that wasn't too dark for Gertie's palette of colors. Gertie walked timidly ahead of Luna and me. She whispered now, "There, in the corner. You see him?"

I looked at a small, nearly black thing in the corner. It had shiny skin that was very bumpy. It sort of looked like a baby alligator, not quite three feet long. It was no alligator. Its head wasn't as long, it was more like a horse head than flat and long like an alligator. Its tail was longer and thinner than an alligator's. Then I looked at the legs. I blinked hard to count the legs. It had six legs. For the love of chocolate, I swear it had six legs.

"What the hell is it?"

"A dragon. He is pretty touchy." Gertie crouched down and held her hand out. "Come here. Come on, sweetie. We won't hurt you."

Slowly the creature crept out of the shadowy corner and came towards us. I could see that it had a frilly fin running along the top of its back all the way to the tip of its tail. It was actually sort of cute, even though I am not much of a judge on dragons. Gertie slowly took a little dog treat from the front pocket of her dress and held it in her open palm.

Luna had decided that she had enough. She dug her claws deep into the skin of my forearm and hissed at the little dragon. I screeched when her claws pierced my skin.

The dragon suddenly stood up on its back legs and held out the middle legs, which unfolded to reveal large shiny dragon wings. It opened its mouth and started making belching sounds. I was quite amused by the little dragon burping at us. I laughed and looked at Gertie.

"Whew! For a second there, I thought it was going to shoot out a blast of fi—"

Then it *did* blast out fire. A blue flame shot out from its mouth. The tip of the flame was only about a foot short of me. I screamed, and once I realized we hadn't been cremated, I ran out of the room. Gertie walked out and apologized profusely. I didn't know what to say.

"What the hell will you do with that thing? There is no way you could sell it as some sort of pet. You will get sued for sure. Once it goes home with a new family, it'll turn the family dog into a plate of barbeque, and then melt the paint off the family car."

"Oh! I forgot to tell you one important detail! The Paranormal Pet Shop is only for witches and other supernaturals. I would never send any of these creatures out into society. I can just imagine how they would be taken advantage of. You know, carnival sideshows, circus acts, science experiments, and those God-awful reality TV shows. At least witches will have an understanding of all this. And they will only take a creature they are comfortable with."

"We should send that dragon to those bitches at the union!"

"Maybe Esmeralda would like it?" Gertie had us both laughing then.

After the frightening experience with the dragon, Gertie introduced me to all sorts of interesting creatures. There were flying monkeys, perfect for the wicked witch in your life. A pair of Sasquatches lounging in the yard. A griffon which was unexpectedly boring since it was asleep the whole time. Just like when you go to the zoo and all the really cool animals are passed out cold and out of sight.

"You know, Gertie, let's say Esmeralda's plan works out and the supernaturals of the world are safe from the union's plans for world domination, or extinction for that matter, then I think all of them would be happy to visit you and find just the right pet. I would probably hold off on creating any new ones right now. Unless of course you don't have a choice, like with those poor Pit Bulls."

"I guess you're right." Gertie nodded. "Why don't we get Luna comfortable, and then we'll zap ourselves into town and get a bite to eat. It's already getting late in the day."

I agreed with her suggestion. I figured I had seen more than enough to make me feel overwhelmed. I needed to keep in touch with reality.

Chapter Twenty One
A Mystery on Girl's Night Out

Gertie and I appeared in Pirate Alley. It's nothing more than a narrow lane that runs alongside the Saint Louis Cathedral, a historic New Orleans landmark. Gertie said she preferred to poof there since there was less chance of being noticed or getting run over. It was just around sundown when we arrived. The heat and humidity was oppressing, but I insisted we walk to where we were going. I immediately fell in love with the unique mix of architecture, the musicians, and street vendors around Jackson Square. And the smells of the wonderful food had my mouth watering.

"Gertie, you have to tell me everything you've found out here in the French Quarter. It's incredible. I don't know if it's just because the Fourth of July weekend is still carrying on or what. It just seems like everyone is enjoying it as much as I am. I have to pick up a book or two about the area, hopefully tonight if there are any shops open."

"Oh, there is almost always something open. I love it here, too! As a matter of fact, I bet that little souvenir shop will have some travel guides or local histories." Gertie quickly changed directions towards a small shop with an Italian flag hanging out front and an Italian name over the door. What happened next was hilarious, but it told volumes of how much Gertie needed to learn about modern slang. She walked up to the little service counter and greeted a very friendly looking and very heavy set middle aged man.

Gertie gave the man a thumbs up and then she said it. "Nice rack!"

"Excuse me, young lady?"

"Nice rack!"

"Whatever. I don't even know why I still work here, putting up with drunken tourists like you all goddamned day. I have a medical problem you know. It's not easy having moobs. You certainly don't help."

"Moobs?"

"What the hell do you want anyway?"

"Why are you so rude? I said nice rack. Happy Fourth of July!"

"You need help, little lady."

"No, I don't think so. Are you offering to help me?" Gertie looked around to see why the man had asked her that.

I had to jump in and save her. I gently tugged at Gertie and led her back out to the sidewalk. "Gertie, why did you say *nice rack* to that man? Was it because of his moobs?"

"At Kelly's parents' party, her dad's brother came up to me. He made a fist and stuck his thumb up. Then he said 'nice rack'. His wife must have been really drunk and swatting at some mosquitoes, she missed them clean and accidentally popped Kelly's uncle right in the face. She knocked the dentures right out of his mouth. Later, I asked him what 'nice rack' and the hand gesture meant, he said it was an Italian greeting for the Fourth of July. Since this little shop here had an obviously Italian name, I thought I should use that greeting. Why? What's the big deal?"

"Oh! That was Uncle Carmine. Yeah, avoid him."

"Why?"

"For one, he's a dirty, old, foul-mouthed, ass-grabber. For two, when he said 'nice rack', he was referring to your boobs. A nice rack means a nice set of boobs to the shallow cavemen we modern women still deal with."

"That old codger! And liar! I bet his wife caught him with that sucker punch on purpose!"

"You can bet on it," I said.

"And what the heck are moobs anyway?"

"Man boobs. Guys with a big, flabby chest. They have moobs. Not a very polite thing to point out about a man, at least to his face. Only do that if he is being a real dick."

"A real dick?"

"Oh, Gertie," I said in an obviously discouraged, yet sympathetic voice. "We have a long way to go with modern slang." I didn't even want to start with the discourse on the use of the word *dick*.

Gertie took us out to the edge of the French Quarter proper to go to a little restaurant that she promised would be authentic, home-cooked style New Orleans food. Along the way, we found another little shop where I picked up two books about New Orleans and the neighborhoods. This time we avoided any embarrassing comments about boobs. We reached a quite old, three story, red brick building on the very busy Poydras Street. I loved the fact that, like so many places I had seen on our walk, it had a second story balcony with a slightly ornate iron railing.

This was the kind of place my dad would refer to as a greasy spoon, meaning no offense to the food, of course. He just meant an eatery with no frills, get down to business meals. A white sign with red letters hung above the sidewalk, *Mother's*. Well, I suppose you almost have to get home-cooked style food there, it is *Mother's* after all.

Gertie, the lover of all animals, the person I most likely assumed would be a vegetarian, apparently had less regard for the lives of lowly sea creatures. "The best thing here is the seafood gumbo. I absolutely love it. It is served with rice. I think I could eat it every day."

"We're friends, right, Gertie?"

"Of course! The best of friends!"

"Okay, since you are the absolute biggest animal lover I have ever met, I figured you would be a vegetarian. Do you eat any sort of meat products, or do you draw the line anywhere?"

"The only meat I eat are eggs, dairy, and seafood. I figure chickens that lay unfertilized eggs are giving those to us so we won't eat them. Cows are sharing their milk because they just love us and want us to be healthy. And seafood—well, I had to pick some sort of meat. When you think about clams, shrimp, and those critters, they seem to be pretty unaware of whether they are going to get eaten or not. What about you? Back in the old days most Jewish families only ate certain foods. Do you follow that, too?"

"No, my family never really did, except in the presence of my grandmother. Actually, I believe that in America less than twenty percent of Jewish families follow kosher dietary restrictions. I don't think I could live without some things like shrimp!"

I followed Gertie's advice and had the seafood gumbo. She was right, it was incredible. I looked at the menu and I knew I would be returning to that place many more times. We talked about more things over gumbo. She was rather interested in what I had to say about Hunter, and she hinted at her curiosity about him, especially his physical attributes and what we did together. I skirted around that and figured out a better idea. I made a mental note that Gertie needed some good girl talk the next time we could both get together with Kelly and Lindsey. That way it wouldn't just be about Hunter and me, but men in general.

We had a great time. We joked and laughed about her use of the phrase that Kelly's uncle, Carmine, had taught her. I explained the common definitions and occasions for the use of the word *dick*. I also explained the use of the name Johnson as a noun when it is used as one more synonym for a very unique male part. Again we had a good laugh at the possibilities of why and how Randy had gotten the nickname Randy Johnson. We were still carrying on with our laughter when we left the restaurant.

I happened to look across to the opposite corner of the street. I recognized someone and I froze in my tracks. I whispered, "Gertie! Look. It's one of the witches from the union board. The Creole woman named Marie. And she's talking to someone, but I can't see who it is. It's a woman." Marie seemed a little nervous as she frequently turned her head to check out her surroundings. The other woman was obscured by a couple of sign posts. I only got a glimpse of a woman in black, with long red hair, and big sunglasses. *Sunglasses? Really? At this time? She is trying to disguise herself. Who could that be? No, it couldn't be Esmeralda, could it?*

Just as I had frozen in place, so did Gertie. She looked at the two women. "That's Marie for sure. Oh my God. She's talking to Esmeralda!"

"Esmeralda? Esmeralda? That dirty double crossing witch! Why would she tell us that she wants to take down the witches on the board and then meet with one of them? This is bullshit. I hate being lied to."

"Should we go over there and just say hi?"

"No. I think we ought to stay out of sight and follow them. Maybe we can figure out what they are up to. Can't you read their minds or something?"

"No. Only the old witches, the original witches can do that stuff. You and I are new witches. In fact, to the old timers we're almost considered half witches or less. We still age normally, unless we are turned into an ice sculpture for a century, and we are pretty much limited to whatever specialty that we somehow came in contact with. Those witches are all *made* witches. I have no idea what that means, except that they refer to themselves as *made* witches."

"Made?" I thought about it. *Where did I hear that word used in that context?* "Oh, Gertie! I get it now. *Made,* like those old style mafia guys that become initiated into the core of those crime families. They get *made.* They become *made* men. They are like the top of the organization. I saw it in a movie once or twice."

"I wonder what they are talking about. Marie is a pretty powerful witch, but she is the nicest of the ones on the board. She is pretty famous, too. You probably heard of her, Marie Laveau, the voodoo witch of New Orleans."

"Really? The name does sound familiar, but I can't say I know anything about her." I looked up her name in one of the guide books I had bought. After I read all about the story of the most famous and powerful voodoo practitioners of New Orleans, I remembered hearing about her before. "That's Marie Laveau? It can't be, it says in this book that she died in 1881. They even have a picture of her crypt with her name on it. I guess a lot of people go there to get some sort of power from her." I showed Gertie my guidebook, which was opened to the page of Marie Laveau.

"No, Leigh. It is her. The witches say that Marie had become so famous that it was drawing too much attention to her magic. The voodoo was something she did, like an act, to throw people off of the idea that she was really a witch. Eventually, people in the city started to look at voodoo from a prejudiced point of view, and she faked her own death to get away from the public eye. She's been living here in the French Quarter ever since, but keeping out of the eye of the public. She even owns a museum and a bar that she has other people run for her. I guess she still gets a pretty good income off of her voodoo."

"They're on the move, it looks like they are heading back into the Quarter, let's follow them. I could just choke Esmeralda for pulling this."

"If there are going to Marie's bar, I'm not going in. There's a mummified kitty on display in there. Just sickening! The poor thing."

And yes, according to the guidebook, Marie's Voodoo Bar had an eerie mummified cat on display in a glass case behind the bar, along with other things to add to the creepy chic décor.

Chapter Twenty Two
Shadowing the Witches

We did our best to keep just far enough away so they wouldn't notice they were being followed. I thought about all of the detective shows on television that had scenes with the private eye or undercover cop putting a tail on the suspect. It seemed to me that in the TV world being a private eye must be a very lucrative industry. It seemed Hollywood assumed it was completely normal for everyone to hire their own detective. Now that I had become an adult, I realized I never met anyone who had hired a private eye. In the real world, people prefer to do their own stalking.

The witches didn't seem to be in much of a hurry. At one point Esmeralda stopped to eye a window display in a leather fetish shop. The two went inside. We positioned ourselves across the street and stayed out of sight. After a while curiosity got the best of us and we crossed the street. Gertie peered in the window while I crouched behind her.

Gertie relayed her observations to me. "I think whatever they have planned involves riding horses. It looks like Esmeralda is trying out a riding crop. Wait! I think that it also involves going to a pig farm. Marie just picked up what looks like an old time hog whip."

"Hog whip?" I remembered it was Gertie making the observations. "Gertie. No, hun, this is a fetish shop, not a livestock supply store. They are checking out kinky stuff." I nudged in next to Gertie and looked inside. Marie and Esmeralda were laughing, and it was obvious they were just playing around. "I think we should get back across the street before they see us." Gertie and I scooted back into the shadows across the street and waited.

The witches came out of the shop, and it appeared they just stopped in to look around. They hadn't bought anything. I became concerned that we were just wasting our time. "Gertie, do you think Esmeralda could be trying to fool Marie into thinking that she is still on their side? Or do you think her and Marie are plotting something that we don't know about?"

"Let's follow them a little longer and see if they give us any clues."

After a short walk, we realized the witches were heading to Café Du Monde, the famous French Market coffee and beignets stand. It is an obligatory stop for anyone visiting the French Quarter, and rightfully so. The witches were soon seated at a little table under the large green awning. I suggested we simply sneak in to see if we could eavesdrop. We both agreed to not get lost in our thoughts, less the mind reading witches picked up our vibes.

We could hear Esmeralda's voice. "I, for one, have no desire to wait any longer. I think it is time to get rid of them."

Marie replied, "You know, its serious business we are talking about. These aren't some trashy little witches off the streets. These are *made* witches, women with powerful connections. They have built the union up from nothing into a machine that can steamroll anyone that gets in their way. Don't let their sophisticated air fool you. They scratched and clawed their way up from the streets. And when I say streets, I'm talking from around the year twelve hundred when witchcraft was forced underground."

"Marie, their reputations exceed their actual capabilities. They can't control the whole supernatural world without having to rely on the magic of those two dimwit baby witches."

I started to get up to yell at Esmeralda. I didn't appreciate her referring to Gertie and me as dimwitted babes. I wanted to give her a scathing verbal takedown that only a pissed off elementary school teacher from Chicago could deliver. Thankfully, Gertie noticed my reaction and held my arm. "Don't. Just don't say it," she whispered.

Now I could hear Marie speaking. "One thing I know about having a frightening reputation is that it is often more powerful than actual threats. If the supernaturals believe it, they will fear it. I know this because that is the premise behind the power of voodoo. It's the same damn thing. Those two young witches have come across some special gifts. I'm glad that I figured out your plot, because I didn't think I could ever do this alone. When we take over the union, we'll have to be sure to take good care of those young rookies. Real good care."

Esmeralda and Marie began to cackle, a very witchy sounding cackle.

I couldn't take it another minute. It was obvious that Marie had uncovered Esmeralda's planned takeover of the union and she wanted in on it. They still needed my magic writing power and Gertie's power to create magical creatures. When they got what they wanted, we would be sleeping with the fishes, as they once said in Cicero. At least that's what Kelly's uncle, Carmine, says. Then again, he's watched a lot of movies, and he is a legendary bullshitter.

We were in a public place. From every old gangster movie I've seen, it was always considered safer to "discuss" any points of contention in a public place. Too many witnesses for anything to go sour. At least I hoped I remembered that correctly. I was too pissed off to be frightened. I had no intention of letting these witches use us and then dispose of us.

"Listen here! You witches—" My building tirade was interrupted by the loud ringtone from my cellphone. It was the song I had selected for when my sister called me. *Girls Just Wanna have Fun, Oh Girls—*

The unexpected ringing startled Gertie who had since crawled under the table for cover. "Sweet baby Jesus!"

"Excuse me." I said as I shut the ringer off on my phone. My sister could talk to voicemail for now. "All right, now where the hell was I? Oh. You witches better both listen and listen well. Gertie and I are not your goddamned pawns to be used and then disposed of later. We know all about what you intend to do with us when you're done. And another thing—"

Esmeralda snapped her fingers and my words were reduced to little squeaking sounds. Everyone else in the café that wasn't a witch was instantly frozen. She leaned back and looked at me with an evil smile, and then she offered me some words of wisdom. If you want to call them that. "It is more shameful to mistrust your friends than to be betrayed by them."

Marie gave Esmeralda an approving nudge on the shoulder. "Ooh, I like that! Well said, Ezzie. Well said. Did you come up with that?"

"I wish. I actually read that from a fortune cookie I opened about forty years ago. I've been dying for a chance to use it."

It was finally time for Gertie to join in. "Well, that doesn't even make sense to me—"

Esmeralda's finger snapped and then she joined me in the squeaky chorus. "No, you listen up Cagney and Lacey."

Marie spoke quietly to herself. "Oh, I miss that show, I just miss it."

Esmeralda nodded towards Marie. "Marie here is joining us on our takeover. Thanks to her, our chances for success have just increased dramatically. As far as your future, neither of us have ever suggested that you would be disposed of. Your words. Not mine. So don't give me any ideas. Now, if you are tired of sounding like mice and you can talk without babbling like an idiot, I'll give you your voices back."

I nodded and our voices returned. "We heard Marie. She said that you two would take care of us real good. That has a very loaded meaning to me."

Marie answered, "Listen, Sweetie, I meant exactly what I said. Literally. We'll take real good care of you for helping out and to make sure you will be available for any favors we need in the future. I just happen to have eight tickets to the Witches Halloween Gala in Salem this year. It is the absolute top of the line bling flingin', hip-hoppin' place to be for all witches, but only a select number get to actually go to it. You want to know what they had in the gift bags last year? A yearlong membership to the Stud Of The Month Club, a trip to Saint Moritz, and some mink slippers, just to name a few."

"That mink slipper business has to stop." Gertie interrupted.

"Pull up a chair, witches. Let's get down to brass tacks and figure out a way to get this over with before the two of you find a way to ruin everything."

We stayed and talked until it was quite late. Our impromptu meeting was very informative. I got a chance to get to know Marie better, and it turned out that I really liked her. She was born in Haiti and came to New Orleans when her father fled from the Haitian revolution, which was happening at the time. Since he was a free man, and an entrepreneur with ties to many powerful people in the French government, it wasn't safe for him to stay in Haiti. Marie's family, and many others that fled to New Orleans, brought with them the ancient religion of voodoo they had once practiced in Africa. It spread throughout Haiti and then to New Orleans. She is a wealth of information on the true power of magic, and she has a great sense of humor as well.

I can't say that I truly like Esmeralda, but I like certain qualities about her. She doesn't take any garbage from anyone. She is proud to be a woman and despite her abrasive personality, she truly is a fighter for the oppressed. I also learned about how the union was formed by Isabel and Hilda. They didn't start out to be evil, power hungry witches, but centuries of oppression against not only witches but women in general had worn down their morals. Everyone is quick to say that the end never justifies the means, but when you are getting taken advantage of repeatedly at every turn, and suddenly you realize you have a powerful way to reverse your fate— well, it can become pretty tempting. I suppose that is how corruption starts in many corners of society.

Of course we devised a plan. It would be secret, simple, and swift. The first phase fell on me. Marie told us that Hilda and Isabel were the most powerful and cunning witches she had ever met. They would have to be captured in order to move forward with the plan. Assassination was completely out of the question. It would be up to me to create a literary character that would become, at least temporarily, the shapeshifter-wolf-vampire-hybrid. I had some ideas in mind. Gertie and I went to get Luna, and we zapped right back to my place.

Chapter Twenty Three
Bound to Forget

It was Monday evening already and I still hadn't moved forward with my assigned task. I paced back and forth in front of my desk. Soon I was joined by Luna. She paced back and forth with me. Gertie had brought along a case of crafting supplies and was concentrating on creating some of her unique art to brighten up my apartment. "Well, I've thought this through, over and over with every scenario. I need a man that I know by name to become Vlad for just this weekend. I can't use Hunter for a number of reasons. And besides, he is up to his neck in police training. I can't use any of the male teachers because I just know it would end up badly for me this next school term. I can't use Derek or Luke because they are the wolf hunters, and of course there's the little detail that Kelly and Lindsey have them busy working over at Lindsey's house this weekend. That leaves just one. You know who."

"Randy Johnson." Gertie said, barely looking up from gluing a foam part to a giant ladybug.

'That's right, Kelly's brother, Randy Johnson. Wait, no. I mean Randy Franchetti. You'll have to call Randy and ask him to stop by. We'll have a talk with him. I have a feeling that he will agree to it."

"When should we do it?"

"You should call him right away and have him come over the day before he has to become Vlad."

"Leigh, I may not be the brightest when it comes to men, relationships, and all that, but why in the world would you want to make Randy into your former book boyfriend? Randy of all people, you know what I mean by that."

"Yeah. I know this is really going to sound crazy, but I am really done with the Vlad of my dreams. I have the Hunter of my dreams now. This will close the door on Vlad forever."

"I guess it doesn't sound crazy. Maybe a little bit, but I think I understand why you want to do this. Couldn't you use Brad, the hot fireman?"

"I thought of him, too. I've never met him. I don't know him at all. Plus, he was already written in as a hot fireman for you. Go ahead and call Randy. Here, take my phone."

Randy readily agreed to come over for lunch on Thursday. Just a relaxing lunch with friends. The less he knew, the better at this point. I would be doing plenty of lying come Thursday. I still had a few logistical issues to iron out, but I would get it figured out later.

Tuesday morning I awoke to my sister's ringtone and I remembered that I hadn't called her back since I missed her last call on Sunday. To my surprise, Sarah and the kids were in town, staying at my parents. Bill had a conference to attend in Chicago. They took the opportunity to use some frequent flier miles and spend some time with Mom and Dad.

I was ecstatic to see my sister. It was a beautiful day, and I suggested that Gertie and I come by and meet up. From there we could all go someplace that the kids would like to see. It worked out fine, the kids wanted to go to the Shedd Aquarium. Before long we were a rowdy gang snaking away through the crowds. Gertie commented on something I had decided not to bring up. I quickly changed the topic. Sarah had placed little backpacks on two of her kids. The backpacks were shaped like monkeys and had a leash attached. Yes, she leashed her kids. Now I completely understand why a parent would do that. I've seen how those kids can be in a crowd. If she didn't have them restrained, she would most certainly never see them again. They didn't listen. I assumed she had raised them to learn a foreign language that neither she nor Bill could speak. If I wasn't at the hospital when they were born, I would have figured she had taken in feral children. There was a possibility there was a mix up at the hospital, I suppose.

Something magical did happen, though. The children were extremely excited at something at the Beluga whale tank. It seemed that somehow the normally pale-skinned Belugas had mysteriously become very colorful. The trainers and marine biologists gathered at the edge of the pool to see for themselves. Each small whale was now a color of the rainbow. I looked at Gertie and she only winked at me.

At some point I cornered Sarah. I followed up on her experiment to rekindle the passion with Bill by reenacting something from her erotic book, *Bound to Forget.* Of course, things had been too hectic, and her entire sex life was still neatly tucked away with half a pack of batteries on a closet shelf. She reminded me that it was the last night in town for her family. When she asked if Gertie and I could watch the kids, I agreed on the condition that they remained leashed. I also requested muzzles, but apparently she left those in Pittsburgh.

The afternoon was slipping away. Gertie and I split off with my two nephews and little niece. The children, as it turned out, were complete angels once they were away from their mother. I reasoned they were reacting to strong vibes of her stress and frustration. The plan was to have them all hang out overnight at my place so Sarah and Bill could make a little progress on putting some intimacy back in their marriage. My parents had to be at an Optimist's Club banquet. To be honest, I have no idea what they do there or why they go there. I don't get it, not at all. My father is the diametrically opposite of an optimist. He had to have lied his way into that club.

The kids had a blast making crafts with Gertie. Luna actually joined in on the fun until the kids decided to rub her belly. After that she disappeared for the night. Children have the unexplainable ability to go from completely healthy to having the symptoms of being ravaged by every microbe known to attack the human digestive track. As my clock struck ten that night, that is exactly what happened. Multiplied by three, it was awful. It was accompanied by the sudden urge to display a fierce case of separation anxiety, times three. I had to promise them that they could go back to grandma and grandpa's house to be with momma. Of course, there was no answer on the home phone, Sarah's cell, or Bill's cell.

I delayed our departure and hoped for things to improve, but it got worse. An hour later I was pulling into my parents' driveway unannounced. Thankful I still had a key, I brought everyone into the darkened living room. The kids immediately passed out asleep on the couch. We heard a sound. Gertie and I strained to listen. It was a strange sound. Like a barking sound. "Ork, ork, ork." Then silence. Gertie figured it was my parents' Chihuahua, Trixie. Why they gave her a porn-star name I have no idea.

We heard it again. "Ork, ork, ork." Then we heard clapping. I turned on a few lights in the living room and

155

we looked around for the little dog. I could hear my sister's voice from the bedroom. I didn't know what she was saying, but her tone was terse and forceful. Suddenly, Bill came charging down the hallway. He was stark naked. He held his hands in front of him. As he got to the lighted living room, we saw that his wrists were handcuffed together in silver cuffs. The surreal scene was topped off by the pink fuzzy material that covered the bands on his wrists. Then we saw that his entire groin was covered in a thick coat of red wax.

He dropped to the floor, writhing in obvious pain. "Get it off! For the love of God! Get it off!"

Sarah rushed out to his aid. She was wearing high heeled, black vinyl boots that went nearly to her knees. She wore a black corset of similar material that only went down as far as her belly button and it cupped under her breasts. It pushed her huge naked boobs out and up in such a way that it looked like a weird Siamese twin bobble head of bald guys with pink noses dancing in front of her.

Gertie just couldn't help herself. "Wow! Hunter's Randy Johnson is a lot bigger than Bill's. A lot bigger."

Sarah was trying desperately to console Bill. "I'm so sorry. I—"

"Urgh! Peel the wax off, please."

"Leigh, Gertie, help me!" Sarah pleaded with us.

We must have looked like we were caught on the tracks with a freight train bearing down on us.

Bill finally noticed us and rolled onto his stomach in shame, as if his large hairy ass was any better to look at.

"What the hell happened?" I asked.

"Your sister! That's what! She decided to play with handcuffs and then pour wax on me. I've heard of that, but I don't think you are supposed to use your mother's giant jarred candle with three goddamn wicks in it. She must have poured a gallon of hot wax on my junk." Bill suddenly pulled his elbows in front of him. Arched his neck up and smacked his palms together as best he could. "Ork, ork, ork."

Sarah yelled at him. "You think you're so funny. Stop being an asshole already. This is not what I meant about pretending to be a hot SEAL."

"I told you, Sarah. I can't, I can't. Ork, ork, ork." Then more clapping. "I can't help myself. I don't understand what's happening to me." Bill looked directly at me with blaming eyes. "This is all your fault, Leigh. All your fault. Goddamn it! Would you PLEASE take these fucking handcuffs off of me, Sarah?"

How did he know? I asked him. "My fault? How can this be my fault?"

"Sarah told me you suggested all of this roleplaying from some filthy book you've been reading. See what comes from that kind of trash? Ork, ork , ork."

Sarah stood there with her baldheaded Siamese bobble heads apparently nodding in agreement.

"Jesus, Mary, and Joseph. It is a good thing those poor babes aren't seeing their parents carry on like you two." Gertie was actually scolding my sister and brother-in-law. "Instead of all of this fussing, shouting, and shenanigans, can't you just go back to the bedroom and diddle your wife, like Leigh's boyfriend does to her? Crimeny sakes man!"

We left Sarah and Bill to deal with the fallout of my magic, once again. When we got in the car, Gertie looked at me and winked. "Witchcraft on your sister?" I nodded affirmatively. "I have no idea how that was *supposed* to go, Leigh. I'm guessing certainly not that way!"

"I'm not too worried this time. I think when morning comes, Bill's bound to forget."

Chapter Twenty Four
One, Two, Three Putsch

"Leigh, I heard you call our plan the big putsch out. What does that mean?"

"Oh, it's a German word for an uprising, like a revolution. I just used it so I could make a little pun."

"Putsch has come to shove, we are out of time now. It's finally Thursday. Are you ready? Did you come up with something to tell Randy?"

"I think I have." Just as I said that, we heard a car pull up. Not only did Randy arrive, but so did Kelly and Lindsey. They walked in, and after Gertie assaulted them with hugs, Kelly confronted me. "Spill it, Leigh. What do you have planned for my brother? I know it's more than just lunch."

I pulled Kelly and Lindsey back to my bedroom while Gertie kept Randy busy chatting in the kitchen. I gave the girls the complete rundown on everything that had transpired since the last time we met. Including my plans for Randy.

I felt like crap. I had wanted to talk to Kelly about my plan first, but I didn't know how she would take it. I assumed she would be upset and typically protective of him. Kelly gave me a chance to avoid an awkward answer.

"Listen, Leigh, Randy is an adult. Whatever it is, he can decide if it's a good thing or not. And I trust you."

Kelly had a concern. "I think it will be fine. Only one thing, how the hell are you going to magically teleport him to Gertie's crazy cat farm? You're not planning to slip him one of those roofies, and then zap him down there while he's passed out, are you?"

"What the hell is a roofie? Leigh! You're not thinking about going on drugs again. Are you?" Lindsey asked.

Kelly looked at her and then at me as if she was already accusing me of drugging her brother. "It's what they call those date-rape drugs that those creeps use to knock girls out so they can attack them and kidnap them. They had an investigative news program about that a couple of weeks ago."

"Oh my God! Leigh! Why would you do that to Randy?"

"Ugh! I was *not* going to drug him! I was planning to *just tell him* what was going on. Everything. I'll have to trust him if I expect him to trust me." Eager to change the subject with the easily distracted Lindsey, I brought up her fire damage. "How is the remodeling job coming along?"

"Awesome! I even had the restoration company hire the roofing company that came out before. That way we have a reason for Luke and Derek to play hotties on a hot roof."

"And spray them down. I know that Stephanie from across the street appreciates it." Kelly added.

We went out to have the talk with Randy. It was pretty easy to convince him since he always thought of himself as an aspiring actor. This would boost his experience and resume. It was an opportunity to play a powerful, yet cultured and wealthy vampire, with the added bonus of being able to shapeshift into a werewolf. The icing on the cake was a visit to Gertie's magically wild mansion, as well as her guided tours of New Orleans after the job was done.

It was now D-day for us. We decided that all of us would go down together, which meant including Kelly and Lindsey, as well as Luna. Before we could leave for New Orleans, we had to gather around my desk. The first thing was to write the story of how Vlad would come back to life, reincarnated into his old self from Randy's body. It worked, but not quite as planned. Instead of the alpha male vampire I expected to see, it was just Randy in Vlad's very typical, gothic vampire tuxedo—for lack of a better word—silk cape, and ivory walking stick decorated with gold and blood red rubies. At least he got fangs.

"This is just fabulous. I love it! Here, feel this material. Have you ever felt anything like it? I think not!" After we obliged and checked out his suit, he went into a performance, or attempted a performance of a vampire. He used all of the old clichés from the old movies. It didn't come off as very convincing. It was still just a little too much Randy and not any Vlad.

"May I introduce my brother, Vlad the Impaler, gayest vampire this side of Transylvania." Kelly was acting as if she had a Romanian accent as she said it.

Randy played up the gay vampire act. "Fang you, fang you very much everyone." We all laughed extremely hard. When the laughter subsided, I just shook my head. *Oh, Vlad, what have I done to you? Are those old witches going to even be the least bit intimidated?* Gertie and I took out our little brooms and transported the entire group to her Pussy Plantation.

They all received a full tour of the mansion, the cats, and the Paranormal Pet Shop. Randy was particularly interested in brainstorming with Gertie, and they hatched a plan that Gertie's plantation would also become a paranormal bed and breakfast. Supernaturals from around the world could visit New Orleans and the Bayou country without having to compromise their usual magic behavior. They could also commission artwork created by Gertie and decorating services provided by Randy's keen eye for the new paranormal chic, not to mention that guests could adopt their own magic pets.

Time had arrived to take the second step. We transported our team down to New Orleans and made our way to the offices of the Witches Union Local 1313. Esmeralda met us in the lobby as planned and hid everyone except Gertie and me. She opened the doors and led us into the boardroom. There, seated at the table were Isabel, Hilda, and Marie.

Marie was the first to speak. "So, young witch, I understand you have completed your first draft of *Four-Bitten Fangtasy*. The fact is, we are not interested in your book. Not at all. We want to meet our new and faithful servant, Vlad the shifter vampire." Marie was playing along so perfectly well that I started to doubt whether she was really on our side.

It was Hilda's turn. "Where is he? I demand to inspect him and see if he is worthy to serve at our bidding."

Esmeralda went out of the room and returned with our new vampire. I held my breath. It was obvious now that Esmeralda was right about Hilda and Isabel. All they wanted was to have an incredibly powerful vampire shifter that they could use as a weapon to control, or even eliminate the rest of the supernatural community. Randy stood silently in front of the board. *Please don't say anything stupid, Randy,* I thought as I watched Randy strike his vampire pose.

Isabel leaned forward and squinted her eyes to scrutinize the vampire. "Who the hell is this?"

"I am Vlad. I am both vampire and werewolf, and I am here to be your loyal servant."

Isabel scoffed, "You sure are not the huge muscular beast that I had hoped for."

"But really, Isabel, his nails are much nicer than yours." Hilda observed.

Randy was so pleased by the compliment that he almost broke character, and I could tell he was about to reply in a typically cheery voice. I had to say something to disrupt everything. "Of course he has nice nails, he is an aristocrat after all. Then again, you old hags wouldn't know true style if it bit you on the neck."

Hilda and Isabel each in turn commanded that he attack Gertie and me. Randy smiled and then in a flash he swooped behind the witches. He bared his fangs and made a wolf-like growl. With the strength of Vlad, he lifted them up. Esmeralda took the opportunity to snatch away their magic wands they used to wield so much power.

Marie shouted, "Now, Gertie!" Gertie closed her eyes, held out her hands, and recited her incantation. There was a puff of smoke and when it cleared, Randy was holding a Cavalier King Charles Spaniel in each hand. One was light pink and white, the other was violet and blue. Marie looked at them and laughed. "Now, there's my little bitches."

That was how the Witches Union was transformed from a power hungry dictatorship into a benevolent union dedicated to protecting all witches, as well as providing assistance to any other supernatural creature in need.

The plan had worked out better than we expected, and now that it was complete, we all went our own separate ways. For now the world was good again. I had my

Hunter to look forward to in a few weeks. Even as I write this, I am drooling over the thought of seeing him in a police uniform.

Gertie now had a burgeoning business plan, thanks to her able friend Randy. He had dropped everything and made an immediate move to the plantation to help her. I know he was saddened by the sudden change from Vlad back to his old self, but Gertie happily offered up her skills. She created a complete replacement Vlad, The Vampire suit for him. I missed Gertie from the minute I crash landed in my coat closet upon my return home. I just had to remind myself that Gertie would be back in Chicago on a regular basis. She had her best friends and a steaming hot fireman named Brad waiting for her to get together with him.

Marie and Esmeralda walked the Quarter with their colorful little spaniels each evening, and they eagerly awaited their regular deliveries of gigolos from the Stud of the Month Club. Thanks to Gertie, they also had their very own flock of flying monkeys.

Kelly and Lindsey are working hard to get something going with Derek and Luke. I am pretty sure I will be called upon to give them another boost towards hot romance. Possibly, I'll have a do-over for Sarah and Bill.

And I can't forget about the Witches Halloween Gala in Salem. All of us will be walking the red carpet, courtesy of Marie that night.

Stay tuned for Leigh's next exciting adventure in Hopeful Leigh.

And....Gertie's escapades in a series of her own, The Paranormal Plantation. Featuring – The Paranormal Pet Shop, The Paranormal B&B, and Randy's Paranormal Chic.

About the Author

Bestselling author, Melanie James spent 14 years as an IT systems administrator before tiring of the hustle and bustle of the technology world. She's doing what she loves by writing steamy paranormal, contemporary and romantic comedy books. Melanie has a Bachelor's Degree from the University of Wisconsin-Oshkosh in Leadership and Development, with a minor in Women's Studies. She is currently working on her Master's Degree in Adult Education at the University of Wisconsin-Stout. She will graduate in the fall of 2014.

She is married to a wonderful man, who supports her dreams and goals. She has two children, three step-children, a beautiful daughter-in-law, and an adorable grand-baby.

You can find the latest information about her books and fan giveaways at: www.authormelaniejames.com

https://www.facebook.com/pages/Author-Melanie-James/14085138327726084?ref=br_tf

Twitter @autmelaniejames.com

Made in the USA
Middletown, DE
22 February 2015